Dark Protector

Moon Shifter Series

Katie Reus

Praise for the Novels of Katie Reus

"This series keeps getting better and better."
—*Joyfully Reviewed*

"Reus has definitely hit a home run with this series... This book has mystery, suspense, and a heart-pounding romance that will leave you wanting more."
—*Nocturne Romance Reads*

"If you like your romance hot with plenty of buildup and a plot that sucks you right in, *Primal Possession* is simply a must read."
—*A Book Obsession*

"You'll look forward to visiting this world again soon!"
—*RT Book Reviews*

"Reus crafts a fast-paced action story... *Alpha Instinct* is awesome: an engrossing page-turner that I enjoyed in one sitting. Reus offers all the ingredients I love in a paranormal romance."
—*Book Lovers Inc.*

"Prepare yourself for the start of a great new series! . . . I'm excited about reading more about this great group of characters."
—*Fresh Fiction*

"A well-plotted, excellently delivered emotional and sensual ride that grabs hold and doesn't let go! . . . Ms. Reus delivers mystery, suspense, and a romance nothing short of heart pounding!"

—Night Owl Reviews

"A strong book full of mystery, intrigue, and a new world to explore. . . . I thoroughly enjoyed this one as I suspect lovers of the paranormal romance genres will do as well!"

—Ramblings from a Chaotic Mind

"If you're looking for a new shifter romance to sink your teeth in, then look no further. *Alpha Instinct* is action-packed with a solid romance that will keep the reader on the edge of [her] toes! . . . Highly recommended for fans of Rachel Vincent's Werecat series."

—Nocturne Romance Reads

"Sexy alphas, kick-ass heroines, and twisted villains will keep you turning the pages...a winner."

—Caridad Piñeiro, *New York Times* bestselling author

"Sexy military romantic suspense!"

—USA Today

"Both romantic and suspenseful, a fast-paced sexy book full of high stakes action."

—Heroes and Heartbreakers

"Reus's passionate and protective alpha-warrior shifters come alive on the page as she continues to deftly expand her intricate paranormal world integrating beings born of myth and imagination... Readers can expect a fast-paced action-packed read including battle scenes and nail-biting suspense."
—Happy Ever After, USA Today Blog

"...a wild hot ride for readers. The story grabs you and doesn't let go." **—New York Times bestselling author, Cynthia Eden**

"Future books in this series are definitely on my auto buy list and I'm looking forward to getting to know the rest of the O'Connor family." **—Feeling Fictional**

"...the characters are heartwarming and energetic; the romance is provocative and seductive." **—The Reading Cafe**

About the Book

He walked away once; he won't do it again.

Wolf shifter Aldric Kazan is no stranger to pain. Since the loss of his mate a century ago, he won't allow himself to fall for someone again—not even the feisty female who stirs things in him that he thought were gone long ago. But as a supernatural investigator, he's forced to team up with the same woman he vowed to stay away from.

She let him in once; she refuses to do it again.

Natalia Cordona refuses to back down from any challenge—even if it means joining forces with Aldric, the sexy and brooding man who won't get too close. Locating missing vampires before a volatile war breaks out seems nearly impossible as the duo struggle with their explosive and undeniable attraction. Now it's up to Natalia and Aldric to trust each other to stop an all-out war from breaking out that would destroy the harmony they've all worked so hard for.

Dedication

For readers who like their heroes a little rough around the edges.

Chapter 1

Arthur kept his posture relaxed as he waited alone in the woods. It was unusually cold for October in upstate New York. Already in the twenties. He wore a thick coat, though not to protect himself from the weather. As a three-hundred-plus-year-old vampire the weather didn't bother him much. But he had on a protective vest. Not that it would help if someone decided to take a head shot.

He was fast though. Faster than a bullet. And...he had to take this meeting. His coven had been feuding with the Kinley lupine shifter pack for over a century. In the past decade things had finally settled down. Partially because over twenty years ago, some foolish members of the supernatural races had decided to go public with the humans about their existence. So now they had to play a lot nicer or risk fallout from the neurotic humans who thought they were all monsters in the dark, waiting to drain them dry.

As if vampires, shifters and other supernatural beings hadn't been around just as long as humans.

It had only been a matter of time anyway, he supposed. With all the technology out there nowadays, one of those vampire or shifter videos on YouTube was bound to be believed.

An icy wind whispered through the bare trees. The moon glowed high in the sky, illuminating the thicket of trees and snow-covered ground.

He didn't bother looking at his watch. The male he was waiting for, the second-in-command to the Kinley pack, was late.

It could be a power play, or the male might have gotten caught in the sudden onslaught of snow not long ago. Arthur was betting on the latter. He would have gotten caught but he'd simply flown over it. Now all was quiet.

Arthur hadn't even told his own mate where he was going tonight. He'd just said he had a meeting. Which wasn't a complete lie, but he didn't like withholding information. A lie of omission was still a lie, especially to a mate. But this meeting was too important to their races. At first he'd been surprised that the male had reached out to him, but once he'd explained he wanted to discuss an ongoing relationship between a member of Arthur's coven and one of the Kinley pack, he'd agreed.

So Arthur had gone to a ridiculous sex club run by one of his people, left his phone and left via underground means so it would be difficult for anyone to follow him. The owner of the club was a friend and had allowed him the use of one of the private exits. He hadn't asked questions either. Which was why they were friends.

At a sudden shift in the air, he straightened, inhaling deeply. The icy air cut at his lungs. Someone was out there, headed his way. A lupine shifter?

But... He inhaled again. Not the male he waited for. He knew that scent. This scent was...not shifter. Not animal either. Something was wrong with the smell—it was chemical, not natural.

Instinctively going into battle mode, he called on his gift, harnessed that inherent ancient power inside him and lifted his body into the air. Not all vampires could fly, maybe five or ten percent, and he was one of the few.

As he glided higher, passing bare tree branches, he swiveled in the air, scanning out below him for—

Something sharp pierced his neck. He automatically reached for the stinging area, his gloved hand pulling away a...dart.

Scanning the trees quickly he looked for the perpetrator. Already his body was slowing, his flight jerky. *There.*

A hooded figure crouched on a pine tree branch halfway up the spindly trunk.

His eyes started to droop, the poison working its way through his veins. The pain silver would inflict wasn't slicing through him, eating away at his insides and organs. He was simply slowing down. Which might mean someone wanted him alive.

No! He refused to be captured like an animal.

A burst of adrenaline poured through him as he ordered his body in the other direction, flying through the trees at a jagged, out-of-control pace.

He couldn't go higher, but he could move forward at least. Except he was moving nearer to the ground every moment, flying into a crash landing no matter how hard he tried to order his body higher.

A branch slapped him in the face as he raced through the biting, whipping air. Under any other circumstance he'd stay and fight. Now he could barely control himself, knew he wouldn't last in hand-to-hand combat.

Rage surged through him. He couldn't believe he'd been taken down by a fucking dart.

He couldn't contact anyone either. Not when they'd agreed to go completely dark.

His only hope was to escape whoever had attacked him, and pray he awoke before the attacker found him. Unless of course he was wrong and even though this wasn't silver, it was something else that would kill him.

He plunged in a sharp vertical drop as whatever was pumping through his system took hold, moving faster and faster through his bloodstream.

He slammed into the icy, white ground, face-first.

He growled, lifting an arm to drag his body somewhere, anywhere. But there was nothing but forest and snow all around him. The very reason he and the lupine shifter had picked this location to meet in the first place.

This lack of control over his body had all his muscles tightening as he strained. His mate might never know what happened to him. That was the only thing he could think of now. He never wanted to cause her an iota of pain. He growled low in his throat, trying to will his body to work.

"It's useless to fight the drug," a female voice whispered from somewhere behind him.

Because of the wind, or maybe because he was quickly losing consciousness, he couldn't pinpoint where exactly. Nothing made sense anymore. He groaned, trying to move away, his claws digging into the snow and earth. He pulled himself, muscles straining, but...he didn't budge an inch.

"That's right, just let go." Her voice was soft, musical. And...familiar.

Another sharp sting hit his neck right before a furious blackness swept him under.

Chapter 2

Natalia stalked across the main yard of the Armstrong-Cordona ranch where she lived with her pack. Once just the Cordona pack, they'd recently united with a pack of incredibly strong males and had a new Alpha: Connor Armstrong.

She didn't bother knocking when she reached Ana and Connor's place. Since they were the pack's Alpha couple, their home was always open unless the front door was locked. Then it was clear the two were getting busy and everyone should stay away.

As soon as she stepped inside she scented cinnamon. Immediately her mouth watered and she followed the scent trail to, of course, the kitchen. Homemade baking was the very reason she'd come here. Because she planned to liberate some cookies to bribe a certain enforcer who was mated to her best friend. Or attempt to bribe the annoying male anyway.

She needed to get off the ranch, like yesterday. And Jayce was her ticket out of here if he would just listen to reason.

The house was quiet, though that made sense for a late morning Wednesday. Most people were out working on the ranch or at one of the many businesses the pack ran.

Today was one of Natalia's days off from the various jobs she picked up and...it gave her too much time with her thoughts. She shoved aside anything that distracted her from her first mission and opened the pantry door. She knew exactly where her cousin kept stashes of the best cookies.

"Hey, peanut." Ana's voice startled Natalia as she stepped into the kitchen.

She spun from the open pantry door, knew she probably looked guilty as her cheeks heated up. "When did you get so good at sneaking up on people?"

Ana grinned and tugged once on Natalia's ponytail. "Since my mate started teaching me just how stealthy I can be."

"You're getting good."

"Will you hand me the slow cooker from the pantry?" Ana asked, moving to the refrigerator.

"Yeah." She picked up the oversized black oval-shaped pot and set it on one of the counters before returning to the pantry.

"You stealing food again?" Ana didn't turn around as she started pulling fresh veggies from the refrigerator.

"What do you think?" Now that her oldest sister had moved out to be with her new mate and her other sister had moved out to live with hers, it was just Natalia and Gloria. And yeah, she could cook but she wasn't the best at baking. Right now she needed something really good.

Setting a bundle of long, uncut carrots on the counter, Ana turned to look at her as she stepped out of the pantry. Natalia had two big containers of cookies in hand. One was for herself—because bribery or not, a girl had to eat.

Ana's dark eyes narrowed ever so slightly. "You planning on eating all those by yourself?"

Natalia plucked out two of the cinnamon sugar butter cookies. The scent alone made her mouth water. They wouldn't make it out of the house. "Maybe." She hadn't really given an answer so that distinct acidic scent of a lie didn't roll off her.

Ana snorted. "Don't give me that. What's going on with you? You've got a mischievous look. Is this about Aldric?"

Natalia snorted. She was not talking about that male. "Please."

Her older cousin watched her carefully. "Connor gets home tonight. Why don't you come by? Maybe we can talk about putting you on a job that will keep you busier? You did really well with..." She trailed off and Natalia figured she knew what Ana was going to say. She'd done really well with Aldric on his bounty hunting assignments. They weren't pack related since Aldric wasn't a member of their pack. But the truth was, Natalia *had* done well with him.

She'd loved the adrenaline and adventure. And she freaking missed it too. Since that jackass hadn't been around in months she was determined to convince Jayce to put her on another mission. Hence the cookie bribery.

Her cousin cleared her throat. "You're ridiculously organized and I know Connor needs a new assistant on an upcoming contract we just got."

Talking about contracts and new jobs was so...normal. Over a year ago they'd dealt with the psycho APL—Antiparanormal League, a bunch of nuts who hated them because they were different than humans—only to deal with more insanity with vamp blood dealing and an evil, dark vampire hell-bent on mayhem and destruction of the world only six months ago.

Now, a year after that first scuffle with the APL, things were so different. Settled, even. There were multiple new matings, three very new pups so tiny and adorable she could hardly stand it, and they had new packmates living on the ranch. Life here was wonderful again. Or it should be.

She cleared her throat. "Ah, maybe. Thank you." She shoved another cookie in her mouth, not wanting to talk about taking on an assistant job. She wanted to get off the ranch, and if Jayce gave her a job, she'd be gone for a while. Exactly what she needed.

Ana covered the short distance between them in two strides and pulled her into a tight hug. Feeling pathetically needy, Natalia set the two containers of cookies to the side and hugged her back tight. As a lupine shifter she needed physical contact as a rule, but now she needed a damn hug.

"Men can be so stupid," Ana murmured against her hair. "I'm so sorry, Natalia."

The words made her feel better. And worse, since her cousin saw right through her. She wasn't fooling anyone, no matter how hard she tried to hide her pain. God, getting off the ranch sounded like the best thing right about now—and she was damn determined to convince Jayce to let her in on whatever his next mission would be. She was a Cordona female and they didn't do freaking pity parties.

Sniffling, she pulled back and managed a half-smile. "Thanks. I'll be fine, I just, ugh, men *are* stupid."

Dark-haired, petite Ana laughed lightly. Even though she was in her late sixties, she looked as if she was in her mid-twenties. Thanks to shifter genes they aged much slower than their human counterparts. "I'm here if you need me."

"I know. Thanks." With a sideways glance Natalia grabbed the two containers from the table and took the batches of confectionary goodness as she exited the kitchen.

Ana just sighed as if she'd expected it, and turned back to the pantry. Natalia knew Ana would have more snacks for the pack hidden so she didn't feel too bad taking them.

Stepping out into the cool fall air, she inhaled the fresh scents. North Carolina was beautiful this time of year, though it was colder than normal.

The pack's homes spread out in a sort of circle from the main house. Recently more houses and cabins had been built to accommodate their growing pack. Though they were on hundreds of acres of property, mainly forest, the homes were close together. Not so close that mates couldn't have privacy, but packs needed to be together for a multitude of reasons, their biological nature being one, and also for safety.

A training facility had recently been built next to one of their parking structures so she headed that way. Jayce, enforcer for The Council—and now a pseudo member of their pack since he was mated to one of her packmates—used it to train his two newest female enforcers.

When she stepped inside she scanned the huge warehouse structure. A huge strip of it was simply mats lined up. There was also a big cage the guys basically used to cage-fight in like complete barbarians. A trampoline was in one corner and along one wall was a bunch of workout equipment—some of which she had no idea what they were. And she didn't actually care. She preferred to get her workouts in wolf form. The place smelled like sweat but it wasn't unpleasant. The earthiness of it pleased her lupine nature.

Most of the males on the ranch used this place frequently now that it had been built. Probably more for male bonding than anything.

She'd taken a few steps in but when she realized she was alone, turned to leave.

"Natalia?"

Turning at Jayce's voice, she saw him striding out from the door that led to the shower area. He wore cargo pants, a T-shirt and as usual his enforcer blades were strapped to his thighs. Her heart rate sped up. Now or never. She just *had* to convince him to take her on his next job. She was about to lose her damn mind here on the ranch. "Hey, just the male I was looking for."

"Everything okay?" he asked, jogging toward her.

She held out a container of what was now only twelve cookies. She should be full but when she was stressed, she ate. "Want one?"

He snorted and shook his head. "You steal these?"

"From Ana." She ate another one, the cinnamon sweetness doing nothing to ease the tension inside her.

"Shameless," he muttered, a half-smile tugging at his normally harsh mouth.

The male was an enforcer for the lupine shifters' Council that governed the packs in North America. Not like the way humans did though. Alphas ruled their own packs, but The Council was kept up to date on the formation of new packs, and if necessary they sent Jayce to mete out punishment to anyone caught breaking their laws.

And Jayce was scary as fuck. Gah, *damn it*, she needed to stop cursing. She'd been trying to cut all curse words out of her vocabulary for the last five months but even in her head she couldn't stop. Vivian had told her she had a potty mouth—which she did. So she was watching herself around the jaguar cub now. Trying to anyway. She couldn't even stop cursing in her head.

"So what's up?" he asked.

Well, stealing the cookies hadn't been pointless because she was hungry, but the truth was, he wouldn't take a bribe anyway. She'd just been hoping to butter him up a little before diving in. *Here goes nothing*, she thought. "Look, I know what you're going to say, but please hear me out before you respond. I want in on your next mission. I did well on the last one—until shit went sideways. But that wasn't really my fault."

She'd accidentally killed an important, ancient vampire. *With one of Jayce's blades.* That had caused a ripple of effects for both their species but that was all water under the bridge now. "And you know I've had experience on other investigations since then. I...need off the ranch, Jayce. Even a small part of a mission would be appreciated." She forced herself to stop before she started begging.

Watching her carefully, Jayce rubbed a hand over the scarred side of his face. He had a wicked-looking scar that formed a crisscross over his left eye. That, combined with his gray gunmetal eyes and the fact that he was five hundred years old? Yeah, scary was a good description. He was one of the oldest shifters in existence, which meant he was very skilled at surviving. The only reason she wasn't scared of him anymore was because she'd seen the way he looked at Kat and their adoptive daughter.

Plus he was Aldric's brother. He'd actually let his brother scar him up centuries ago because Aldric had been in mourning. Aaaaannnd at that thought, the cookie turned to cardboard in her mouth. The reason the male had been in mourning had been because his mate had been killed.

Natalia didn't think Aldric was over her, would probably never get over her death. Something she didn't want to think about now. She'd wasted enough time letting him take up space in her head. She was moving on, and taking on a new mission away from the ranch was the best way for her to do that.

"I'm heading out soon on an investigation with Kat. I could use an extra person I trust as part of the team. You're in if you really want."

She blinked. She'd been so sure she'd have to convince him. "For real?"

"Yep. You'll need to clear it with Connor, but I think you're perfect for this. It's in upstate New York. We'll be attending a party with a feuding vamp coven and lupine pack. The Clifton coven and Kinley pack." He paused, as if waiting for her to recognize the names.

She'd never heard of either the coven or pack, but that wasn't unusual. Not considering how insular supernaturals could be. "I'm in."

He nodded once. "Good. You'll be one of my eyes and ears—like at the club thing we did in Winston-Salem."

That was the night she'd met Aldric for the first time—and the night she'd killed someone for the first time. *Ugh.* She didn't want to think about that now. The guy had deserved to die so she didn't feel guilt over it. Not truly. "I've been begging you for months to take me on another mission. Why the change?"

"I think you'll work well with the partner I have picked out for you."

If she was going to get this opportunity, she wasn't going to turn it down. Not when spending time away from the ranch and having some adventure was exactly what she'd been craving. "Who's my partner?"

"A vamp. You'll like him. He's easy to work with."

There was only one thing left to ask. "When do we leave?"

Chapter 3

Jayce pushed open the door to the house he shared with Kat. There was an underlying scent of roses teasing him—his mate's scent. It was still surreal that he was mated at all, much less to a woman better than any fantasy he could have imagined. The scent was strong enough to let him know she was home even if he couldn't hear her moving around upstairs.

It made him edgy, needy. Something he was still getting used to after only ten months. Though he'd known her longer than that, had been in love with her longer too.

The first time he'd met her he'd wanted her, craved her with a need he hadn't expected. He'd wanted to push her away, push away anyone who could make him *feel* like that. He'd been rude and offensive to her—and she'd laughed in his face, calling him a little puppy.

Her words had been like a challenge, one he hadn't been able to resist. So he'd chased after her until he'd caught her. Then he'd been stupid enough to let her go, but luckily the gods or God or someone had allowed him to have her back. He'd almost lost her because of his own stupidity, then at the hands of an evil group. Never again.

He'd never let her go. The female owned him. She was his heaven.

"Hey, you," she said, jogging down the stairs, her long black hair loose around her shoulders. "Leila's over at December's. She's going to babysit tonight so Liam and December can get away for some grownup time."

Translation—he and Kat got grownup time too. He growled low in his throat, pleased at the thought. It didn't matter that they made time for each other—he was always ready for her.

Her pale blue eyes went pure shifter as she paused halfway down the stairs. With a wicked, knowing grin, she turned on her heel and raced back up the way she'd come.

Daring him to chase her.

He loved chasing her. They both loved when he did. Moving with lupine speed he sprinted after her, his feet barely touching the stairs until he stood in the doorway of their bedroom.

Their bedroom.

The first they'd ever had that was all theirs. Not his or hers, but a home they lived in together. As a family.

She was stretched out on her back on the pile of giant fluffy blankets they kept in front of their fireplace. Her hands were behind her head as she stared at him, her wolf still in her gaze. "You must be getting old," she murmured. "I beat you this time."

"Old?" He stalked toward her, all the muscles in his body pulled taut. His erection was already shoving insistently against his pants, the mere scent of her pushing him to the edge.

"Mm hmm." Her eyes flicked back to human, the humor there making him smile even as he felt primed for her. This female completely undid him.

He stripped off his shirt and shoes before he knelt in front of her. His pulse was an erratic beat. "Why are you still dressed?" he rasped out.

"Waiting for my mate to take care of that." There was a haughty note to her voice that had his cock straining even more. He could be patient when he wanted—except with her.

She didn't move other than to spread her thighs wider as he slid in between her legs. He reached for the button of her tight jeans and slid the denim down her legs. She should never, ever wear clothes. At five feet nine inches, it seemed she had miles and miles of smooth, toned legs. A scrap of bright pink material covered her pussy and he knew she'd have on a matching bra.

His mate liked to wear pretty things and he'd had to stop tearing them off her. Sometimes it was simply easier to flick out a claw and slice through the barrier between her body and him. But...he'd learned to be a little more civilized for her. Or at least feign it. Because he would do anything for his Kat.

She rolled her hips once, arching off the blankets in a lazy, sensuous motion. "Too slow," she whispered, her eyes full of a hunger that mirrored his own. It had only been two days since he'd last had her, but it felt like a lifetime.

In seconds she was completely bared to him, his beautiful, strong mate. Long and slender, she had a hint of curves he couldn't resist running his hands over. Not that he wanted to resist. He wanted to consume her right now. With his callused hands, he cupped her breasts, teased her light pink nipples with his thumbs.

The scent of her arousal filled the room, making his primal side shove to the surface like a battering ram. "How do you want it?"

Her cheeks flushed, her eyes went wolf again. "Surprise me."

When she said that she usually meant she wanted it a little rough. Right now he needed to take the edge off first. Bringing her to orgasm would do that for him. He needed to please his mate on a bone-deep level. Something about being bondmates did that to males. They had to take care of their females in every way. And he loved doing it.

Without warning he buried his face between her legs. She let out a yelp of surprise before one hand gripped his head. He normally shaved his head but he'd grown out a little buzz for her because she said she liked the way it felt against her fingertips.

She tasted sweet and all his. That primal thing that lived inside him was right at the surface, teasing and tasting her.

"Jayce." The way she gasped out his name was like a prayer, all needy and desperate.

His tongue delved into her oh-so-slick folds. She was soaked for him and they'd barely started. He teased her over and over before focusing solely on her clit. The little nub was swollen and sensitive.

She jerked against him the harder he stroked her clit, making nonsensical sounds. He could drown in her taste, in her, and die a happy shifter.

There had been a time when he'd been sure he'd lost her for good. At that thought he increased his efforts, pressuring her clit more than normal just as he slid two fingers inside her.

With another surprised yelp she started coming, as he'd known she would. He'd learned exactly what she needed to find release, loved pushing her over that edge. As her inner walls tightened around him, milking his fingers harder and harder, her thighs clenched around his head and she called out his name.

He relished the pressure, savored the taste of her climax on his tongue as she rode through her release. Finally, he pulled back to look up the length of her body.

She looked down at him with a sultry, sated expression as her legs fell, boneless, to the blankets.

Hard and aching, he crawled up her body, caging her underneath him. When they were face to face she smiled up at him, cupping his cheek with one hand as she wrapped her legs around his waist.

Unfortunately he was still dressed. Moving quickly he shoved his pants off before caging her in again. With nothing between them, he got exactly what he wanted.

He didn't need to guide himself with his hand, instead just positioned his cock at her entrance and slid fully inside her.

Gasping, she arched her back as he filled her.

His jaw tightened and his balls pulled up harder as she clenched harder around him. He kept his gaze pinned to hers, watching her as he remained in place.

Staring up at him, she slid her hands over his chest and stroked his shoulders. "I missed you today," she murmured, rolling her hips against him.

He was beyond words at this point, and nipped her bottom lip between his teeth before devouring her mouth. She met him stroke for stroke, her tongue delving past his lips, just as hungry for him as he was for her.

"Move," she groaned against him, the word muffled. But he understood it.

Gladly. He began thrusting, slamming into her in rough, hard strokes. When she'd been human he'd been more careful with her. Now, they could both give in to their primal urges.

Her nails scored down his back as he slammed into her, over and over. It didn't take him long to reach the edge but he held back, wanting to savor the feel of her tight sheath milking him.

He loved the way she took him, as if they'd been created just for each other. Latching on to one breast, he sucked a nipple into his mouth. She arched again, digging her fingers into his back.

Her inner walls grew slicker, clenching even tighter. She was close, ready to climax again. He craved it, to feel her orgasming around him.

Reaching between their bodies he tweaked her clit, rubbing it in a tight little pattern guaranteed to push her over the edge once more.

"Jayce!" She buried her face against his neck only to pierce his skin with her canines.

There was no pain, only pleasure as she marked him. Another reminder that he belonged to her as much as she did to him. He let go of his control then, his own orgasm slamming through him, piercing all his nerve endings as pleasure pummeled his body.

When they both collapsed against the blankets, he rolled to his side, instinctively pulling her to him. She laid her head against his chest, her breath skating against his skin in uneven rasps.

He stroked a hand down her hair and spine. Inhaling, he let her scent fill him. She was his.

"What time does Leila come back?" he asked sometime later. He wasn't sure how long they'd been lying there. Didn't really care as he held Kat in his arms.

She laughed lightly, no doubt knowing why he asked. "Not sure."

"Natalia asked to come on our mission Friday," he said abruptly. Saying yes to her hadn't been an impulsive move. Not exactly. But there were others he could have asked. Those with more experience and training. Natalia had been so damn eager though and the truth was, she would do a good job. That was never in question.

Kat lifted her head, propping her chin against her hand as she looked at him. "You said she was too young—even though we're pretty much the same age."

Part of him still didn't like taking Kat on missions with him, but he'd rather have her with him than leave her behind. And the only way for her to grow into her strength, to learn how to truly fight, was to work with him. "I changed my mind."

His mate snorted. "Are you playing matchmaker at your age?"

He pinched her ass. "What's up with the age jokes?" he mock growled.

"I just like messing with you," she murmured, nipping his chin lightly.

He loved that about her. She'd brought so much into his life, including laughter and playfulness, something he'd missed for centuries. "No. I think she'll be perfect for this job. But I want my brother to find what we have." He hated seeing his brother alone. It was like part of Aldric had died all those centuries ago—until he'd met Natalia. Jayce wouldn't let his brother be a dumb-ass and let her slip through his fingers. So if that meant he brought Natalia in on a job that Aldric just happened to be part of?

Kat's expression softened. "Just when I think I can't love you any more than I already do. And I agree. God, what is wrong with him?" she muttered.

Jayce didn't respond. Aldric had lost his pregnant mate centuries ago. The loss had changed him irrevocably. Since he'd met Natalia, however, Aldric had seemed as if he could be fucking happy again. Then he'd gone on a mission and just decided to not come back. He'd been gone over five months and though he was in touch with Jayce and Kat, Jayce knew that Aldric had simply cut Natalia out of his life.

Jayce understood what that was like, how much it hurt. Aldric had done the same damn thing to him centuries ago when he'd lost his mate and gone a little mad. But he'd seen the change in his brother since Aldric had let Natalia into his life.

"She doesn't ask about him anymore. Hasn't in months." Kat's voice was quiet.

Jayce nodded, figuring as much. "I didn't tell her he'd be there."

Kat lifted her eyebrows but didn't respond, just laid her head back on his chest. After a few minutes, she slid a hand down his stomach and grasped his hardening cock. "Think we have time for a quickie before we're not alone anymore?"

He had her pinned flat on her back before she'd finished the question. The answer was always a yes.

Chapter 4

"I don't want to go to this fucking party," Ursula snarled, showing her fangs. She stomped a heeled foot against the entryway of her grand foyer before taking a vase and throwing it at a wall.

Using quick reflexes, Aldric caught it, sighed and put it back on the pedestal she'd grabbed it from. He focused on her. "Then you wish me to stop investigating your mate's disappearance?" The truth was, he wouldn't stop no matter her answer. He'd been hired to do a job. Not to mention Arthur was his... maybe not *friend,* exactly, but he respected the male.

Aldric would find him or find what had happened to him, if he was indeed dead. Though according to Ursula he wasn't, because she could feel her mate's existence still in the world. Too bad she couldn't tell Aldric where exactly. Because his job could never be easy.

"Don't be an ass! I didn't say I wasn't going. Just that I didn't want to go." She smoothed a hand down her elegant black dress. Her reddish hair, streaked with gold, was pulled up into a twist at her neck.

"You done with your tantrum?" He kept his voice mild, knowing it would annoy her enough to start behaving. She was almost as old as him and normally the epitome of control. He could understand her emotional state right now though. Her mate was missing and she was worried about him. But Arthur was smart and would find a way to survive if at all possible. Ursula just needed to remember that.

Jaw clenched tightly, she nodded and turned her back to him, showing an expanse of bare skin. He took one of the recorders she'd be wearing and slid the jeweled piece into her hair. Even to a trained observer, no one could see that it was a recording device. She was also wearing a microscopic recorder in a necklace he'd provided her with. Technology was an incredible thing.

"It's secure," he said, dropping his hands. When his cell phone buzzed in his pocket, he pulled it out, scanned the message. "Jayce and his mate are already there." Jayce, Kat, a vampire named Niko and some others, Jayce had said, would be eyes and ears at the party as well. Aldric didn't tell Ursula that, however. She didn't need to know who else would be there listening and recording just as they would be.

He'd taken this job at the request of the Brethren, a group of four ancient vampires who more or less governed vampiric kind across the globe. They liked contracting Aldric because he was a shifter and impartial. And Aldric liked the money and purpose, though he'd have taken this case pro bono simply because it was Arthur missing.

"How on earth did the enforcer get an invite to this party?"

He noticed she called Jayce 'the enforcer' and not his brother. Aldric lifted a shoulder, not bothering to answer. She'd pretty much answered her own question anyway. Jayce was a fucking enforcer for The Council of lupine shifters in North America. He went wherever he wanted. All he'd had to do was reach out to the Kinley Alpha and tell him he wanted to attend with some friends. Not all Alphas would have acquiesced so easily but Jayce was actually friends with this one. It made things easier for everyone.

"What's his mate like?" she asked, picking up her clutch from the foyer table as he opened the front door.

He might like Ursula well enough, but he wouldn't tolerate anyone asking questions about the only family he had. Family he'd cut out of his life hundreds of years ago because he'd been a hurting, foolish wolf. He hated all the time they'd lost together. Had no one to blame but himself. Things were still awkward between him and Jayce occasionally. It was one of those things he knew would change only with the passage of time. Or he hoped it would.

A sleek black luxury car was waiting for them, the driver standing alert next to the open back door. Ursula slid in first, Aldric following behind.

"She's tall, beautiful," he finally answered. Words that would give away nothing about what his brother's mate was truly like. She was fierce, incredibly loyal to his brother and loved him to the point she'd die to protect him. Those were the traits that really mattered. Thinking of his brother and his mate just reminded him that he'd been away from the Armstrong-Cordona ranch for too long, though he'd seen his brother in town under the guise of 'meetings.' A few times he'd simply asked Jayce to meet him at a bar for drinks, something that seemed so benign and normal. He savored the times it was just the two of them.

Ursula snorted. "You tell me nothing with those words."

Aldric gave her a sharp look. "It's all you'll get. I'm here at the request of the Brethren." *So don't forget it* were the unspoken words.

He rolled his shoulders once, trying to shove back errant thoughts of a certain female he'd been trying to forget for months. He could return to the ranch, get his fix of her, just see her once, draw in her addictive scent. But he needed distance from the sweet wolf. She was thirty, but that was young by lupine standards. Young by *his* standard. Natalia Cordona—petite, feisty and a female he wanted with a desperation that disturbed him. He loved her thick, espresso-colored hair with just the faintest tint of caramel. He'd fantasized about running his hands through it as he claimed her mouth or as she rode him.

He was almost certain she was a virgin. Something else he couldn't deal with. She was too sweet, too… Just not for him. That was what he told himself anyway. He hadn't been able to protect his first mate so very long ago. He didn't deserve another. And with Natalia he wouldn't settle for anything else. His wolf wouldn't allow it. He couldn't bear the thought of losing her either.

So he'd stayed away for as long as he could. His wolf was getting restless though. Demanding, clawing, making him edgy in a way he'd never felt. His wolf wanted to go after her and didn't understand why he was staying away.

"I'm sorry," Ursula murmured, pulling him back to the present. Her gold-amber eyes flashed with pain as the driver pulled away, heading down the long, winding driveway. "I'm just looking to make mindless small talk. I can't stop thinking about Arthur, where he is, if he's hurt. If he's…" She swallowed hard.

Going against his instinct, he reached out and patted her hand gently. "I will find him."

She nodded tightly, looked out the window.

Many members of the Clifton coven lived in the biggest mansion in this sprawling vampire-only neighborhood in upstate New York, but Ursula and her mate lived in their own place with a small staff. Close enough to their leader, but far enough away that they weren't inundated with their coven members' lives. Some vampires craved solitude while others wanted what wolves and other shifters did, a pack. Though they'd never admit it.

With a few minutes to kill, he pulled out his cell phone to indulge in something he shouldn't. Tilting his phone away from prying eyes, he pulled up a picture of Natalia he'd snapped when she hadn't known he was watching.

Sitting on top of one of the fences surrounding a horse pen, her dark hair was pulled up in a ponytail showing off the smooth, tanned skin of her cheeks. A blue and white scarf that one of her sisters had made was wrapped around her neck and wisps of errant hair were flying with the wind.

Her smile was brilliant and heart-stopping, her dark eyes filled with joy. She'd been laughing at something one of the pups had done, her enjoyment pure and infectious. He'd been unable to stop watching, staring. Soon, just being around the female had become an addiction. He'd wanted her too much, would have done anything to have her.

So he'd done what he seemed to be best at. He'd run.

***

Ursula had a relaxed smile on her face as she linked an arm through Aldric's. He didn't want anyone touching him—anyone other than Natalia.

But they would stay together during this party.

"You're doing perfect," he murmured at a subvocal level only she would hear.

Her smile remained in place, perfectly pleasant even though this had to be difficult for her. To be at a party while her mate could be suffering or worse. But she needed to be here. And at her age, she'd clearly perfected the ability to fake it, to appear calm when she was anything but. He could practically hear the screams inside her, the rage at not knowing where her mate was, if he was being harmed.

"This will be a big help," he continued, wanting to do anything he could to keep her calm. Only she would understand what he meant, but he needed to drive the point home.

Ursula was here while her mate was missing. Almost no one was aware that Arthur had been taken except Elian Clifton, the leader of the Clifton coven, and of course the Kinley Alpha and a few other trusted high-ranking members of the coven and pack. Aldric would be reviewing tonight's recordings not only for audio but for visuals.

If someone appeared startled to see Ursula at a party, he would make it his business to find out who they were and why they were fucking surprised to see her. Because only the person who'd taken Arthur should be shocked at Ursula's presence.

Of course, he could come away with nothing for all his trouble, but that was simply how investigations went. He had to chase down every lead.

"I hope so." Her voice was brittle, in contrast with her almost serene expression.

As they passed a scantily clad server with pink champagne, he took two flutes, handed one to her. They needed to appear to be at ease, to blend in. He wasn't a member of either the coven or pack, but he knew enough people here that it was common knowledge he was friendly with Arthur and Ursula.

"Ursula, who is your delicious friend?" A blonde female in a skintight crimson dress looked him up and down, her gaze calculating and hungry as she spoke to the woman on his arm.

Aldric had turned away, pretending to already be bored by the female's presence, when he heard a whisper of conversation.

"Masking scents is becoming easier and easier," a male voice murmured.

Aldric casually scanned the clusters of people, half-listening to Ursula asking the blonde benign questions. There were so many conversations going on, so many people, it was difficult to filter what he wanted to focus on.

"It's not the masking that's interesting... If... duplicate... scent." He heard bits and pieces as raucous laughter filled the air.

"Excuse me," he murmured to Ursula. Without waiting for a response, he stepped around a group of four vampire males seriously debating the merits of fantasy football. It was the strangest thing he'd ever heard vampires talk about.

After moving around them, he narrowed in on two males, both vampires, crouched together talking intently. Both males had touches of gray in their hair, telling him they'd been turned later in life. The one on the left had rich brown skin and laugh lines around his eyes and mouth. The other had fewer lines and an olive coloring, his features hinting at Mediterranean heritage. Aldric memorized their faces even as the tiny recorder on his jacket captured their images.

He would be talking to them soon. Their conversation could be nothing, but hearing two vampires discussing duplicating scents was something he would follow up on, regardless of this case or not.

Moving casually, he turned back to see Ursula striding toward him. She looked annoyed at him, but it didn't matter. He'd come here to do a job.

As she reached him, he scented a familiar combination of cherry blossom and vanilla somewhere just out of reach. Somewhere close, but not close enough.

Natalia was here.

Chapter 5

"This place is amazing," Natalia murmured to Niko, the vampire whose arm she was holding on to, as she stared out the car window at the sprawling estate. Her own pack had money and property, but they didn't show off their wealth to this degree. Not even close. She wondered if it was a vampire thing to be so ostentatious.

It had taken five full minutes simply to make it down the long, curved driveway. Now they were waiting in line for the valet.

"They're one of the wealthiest covens I know of." His voice was gravelly, raspy. Jayce had told her that before Niko had been turned into a vamp, someone had slit his throat. He hadn't died but after he'd been turned, that voice hadn't changed. Apparently he was as old as Jayce, something she believed. There was too much knowledge in his dark eyes. "They invested well and likely hid much of their money, and were ready when it was time to come out to humans."

Niko was shockingly sweet for a vampire. Of course she hadn't met many, other than one of her packmates' mates, who she liked. The other vampires she'd come in contact with, however, had tried to kill her. On multiple occasions.

"As soon as we're out of this vehicle—and even once we've left the party—we're in character." His voice was quiet.

"I know." He was a lot older than her—by like five hundred years—and he simply wanted to make sure she was ready for tonight.

She was his date for the party. After they left later, he said he couldn't be certain that his vehicle wouldn't have been bugged so they were to simply act normal. And Niko was operating independently from Jayce. He'd purposefully garnered his own invitation to this event.

Her stomach tightened as they waited in the valet line. The Italian Renaissance-style estate had over two hundred and fifty rooms, and two gardens, one with a maze she wanted to see. The eight golden domes spaced out evenly along the top of the home seemed to glitter under the moonlight. Anticipation hummed through her at what the interior would be like.

Next to her, Niko chuckled. "I can smell your excitement."

"Is that bad?" She'd probably be one of the youngest here, if the report on both the shifter pack and vampire coven attending was any indication. Maybe the people here were used to this kind of lavishness. She was definitely not.

"No, it's good. I guarantee you will get propositioned. You have a sweetness about you. And you're young. Many of the older shifters will... want you. The vamps too."

"But I'm a shifter. And I thought the coven hated shifters."

He shot her a sideways glance as they crept along. "No, they're just at war—sort of—with the Kinley pack. Doesn't mean they don't intermingle with shifters."

"So how did you get an invite to this?" Jayce hadn't said and she was curious.

Niko lifted a shoulder. "I'm old and know many, many vampires. I just contacted a former lover and mentioned I'd be in the area. After that, getting an invite was simple."

She blinked. "Won't she care that you're bringing a date?"

"No. We were together centuries ago. Though she did ask if you'd be up for a threesome." Amusement laced his words.

Natalia would have been surprised by the statement if not for Jayce's rundown of what this party would be like earlier. "What did you say?"

His laugh was full-bodied. "She knows I don't share. I think she was testing to see if I'd changed in my old age."

He appeared as if he was in his thirties, but that meant nothing to supernaturals. "I thought vampires were all sort of hedonistic."

"Many, many are," he murmured as they reached their destination.

"Should I bring my coat?" She'd worn a simple but elegant ruby-colored dress that fit her like a second skin. She'd never have bought anything like it for herself but Jayce had given it to her, said this was her 'armor' for the evening. She was pretty candy on Niko's arm. She had a covert recorder placed in one of the jewels on her three-layered necklace. She wasn't sure if it was costume jewelry or not—and didn't want to know in case it was real.

"Only if you want," he said as two vampires opened their doors for them.

She decided to leave it behind. Upstate New York was chilly this time of year but she was a lupine.

Niko rounded the vehicle to meet her and she immediately slid her hand through his arm and loosely held onto him.

For the briefest moment a familiar scent carried on the breeze, but she must have imagined it. If Aldric was going to be here tonight, Kat would have told her.

Still... That aroma that reminded her of a dark, wintery forest lingered until they stepped inside. Great, she chided herself. Now she was imagining things.

"What is it?" Niko murmured as they ascended the stairs to the main doors where two women wearing matching sparkly pink slip-style dresses that were reminiscent of the nineteen twenties stood.

They each held a tray with champagne flutes, some with actual champagne, some with a dark liquid that was definitely blood. Niko passed but Natalia plucked a glass of bubbly pink champagne from a tray, smiling her thanks to the woman. "Nothing," she said as they entered the grand foyer. Classical, calming music filtered out from somewhere. "Just nerves."

He slid an arm around her waist and even though she wished she was with another male, Niko's presence was a comfort as they turned into what was a very huge ballroom. Ivory, gold and marble swathed the lavish space. Half a dozen marble caryatid statues were visible and she wondered how old they were, given the clear wealth of this place. The bit of the marquetry inlay she saw on the floor as they walked was breathtaking.

The room was filled with shifters, vampires, and even some humans, all elegantly dressed, most of the women wearing glittering jewelry and the men in various style of dress. Some in tuxedos, some in...cargo pants and T-shirts with weapons strapped to their thighs or across their backs. She shouldn't be surprised, not since this was a supernatural party. Shifters sometimes just didn't give a fuck about a dress code.

The crowd was too thick to see if Kat and Jayce were here and she wasn't supposed to look for them anyway. She and Niko were just supposed to blend into the crowd and record. Right now the coven throwing this party and the shifter pack in attendance were on the cusp of finally signing a peace treaty and putting centuries of animosity behind them.

Unfortunately one of Elian Clifton's most trusted, senior vampires was missing. Not everyone knew it, but if he was gone much longer there would be trouble.

And no treaty.

While it didn't technically affect Natalia's own pack, if the Kinley pack and Clifton coven went to an all-out war, it would eventually draw the attention of humans and be very, very bad for other shifter packs and vampire covens. They were no longer able to live as insularly as they once had. Now that they were 'out' to humans, the actions of one pack or coven could affect the way humans viewed all of them. It was a delicate balance of survival they played.

Niko leaned closer to her, pressed a gentle kiss to her forehead. That was one of their signs, that she needed to be ready for something.

Almost as if on cue, an attractive vampire couple approached them. "Niko, you naughty boy," the female murmured, kissing him on the cheek before turning to Natalia, her smile welcoming and... a little flirty. "He hasn't been to a party with us in ages," she continued, her accent delicately French.

Her skin was a pale cream where her partner's was dark, almost ebony. He gave her a more polite smile, but there was still clear interest in his gaze as it swept over her, as if he was imagining her naked.

"Natalia, this is Arlette and Henri." Niko's voice was low but she heard it well enough over the din of voices and music.

"We have a room here if you two are interested," Arlette said, her smile pleasant.

Wow, they really didn't waste any time. Both Jayce and Niko had warned her to be ready to be propositioned but she'd assumed it would happen after some conversation. Or something. Natalia could tell that Arlette was the alpha in this relationship. The male seemed almost passive, but her wolf sense, more than anything, told her that this female was in charge.

Before she could respond, Niko let out a low growl that didn't exactly make her hackles rise, but she felt the power thrumming from him. "You two know better." His tone was almost admonishing. He tightened his grip around Natalia, sliding his hand around her waist and cupping her ribs right under her breast.

She appreciated that he didn't go any higher. She'd known they'd have to act as lovers tonight but that didn't mean he'd get liberties she wasn't willing to give. Something she'd made clear with him earlier. He'd given her a look that said he hadn't planned to do anything anyway. Which made her like the male even more. Not in a sexual way, not even close. But...he really was just a nice male.

Arlette laughed, surprising Natalia. "I had to try. One of these days we will get you into bed with us." Her blue eyes twinkled mischievously.

In response Niko bent down, gently raked his teeth against Natalia's neck. The act was intimate but one she'd been prepared for. He was telling everyone here that she was his. At least for the moment. "Not tonight," he said, in what Natalia thought was an indulgent tone as he raised his head and looked at Arlette.

A low growl to her left made everything inside Natalia go still. This was supposed to be a peaceful party, but her animal instinct told her danger was near. Too many scents surrounded her to be able to sift through all of them.

Swiveling, she lost her breath.

Aldric stood ten feet away from them, his grayish-green eyes pure wolf. She felt as if she'd been sucker punched as she drank in the sight of him. She felt greedy, as if she couldn't get enough of seeing him in the flesh. A little over six feet tall, the male was broad and muscular, with so much strength humming through him it was almost a palpable thing. His dark hair was still military short, a soft buzz she'd fantasized about running her hands over more than once. Even though he was a shifter and healed quickly, scars still nicked all over his body. Savagely handsome with a wicked edge to him, he was the type of male it was hard to look away from.

Right now, he was staring at Niko with a look that promised death on the near horizon.

Chapter 6

Aldric tried to shove his wolf back down but failed. Miserably.

Natalia stood next to a male vampire. One Aldric knew. Liked. But the male's hold was possessive, protective, and Aldric's primal side was barely controlling the urge to kill.

Natalia stared at him, dark eyes wide, clearly surprised to see him. She wore a bright red strapless dress that made her stand out, highlighted her natural beauty. It wrapped around her lithe body, leaving little to the imagination. The full mounds of her breasts looked as if they were about to spill out. Which made his wolf all sorts of possessive. He wanted to strip it off her, to claim her—mark her—so that this fucker knew she was his.

So that *everyone* knew she was his.

He'd saved her once, months ago, from being killed by two asshole vamps who thought they were avenging their maker's death. They'd become friends, but he'd wanted so much more it clawed him up inside. He'd gotten glimpses of sexual interest from her occasionally but it was so muted it was difficult to tell.

Until the last day he'd seen her. She'd wanted to come with him on a bounty hunting trip and he'd told her no. He'd caged her in against her front door and had to restrain himself from claiming her mouth. Because he wouldn't have stopped at kissing.

He'd have taken what he was certain she would have freely offered. If she'd have told him no he'd of course have backed off, but he'd scented pure, unbridled hunger from her that morning.

It had taken him off guard. The scent had been addicting and he'd been at his breaking point where she was concerned. He'd had to walk away from her, from the possibility of them. He hadn't been able to protect his first mate, wasn't nearly good enough for Natalia. Leaving had been the only option.

Now, to see her here with another male, a male who had his hands on her... It was too much for his wolf to handle.

"Aldric." Next to him Ursula gently touched his forearm.

He jerked his gaze to her and snapped his teeth—and realized his canines had descended as well as his claws.

The female looked at him with shock and just a touch of fear as she took a step back.

Natalia tried to push in front of the vampire... to protect that fucker? Aldric growled even deeper.

The male shoved Natalia behind him at wicked-fast speed. "What the fuck is your problem?" Niko rasped out.

Aldric was vaguely aware that much of the chatter around them had dimmed, with only a few people whispering. The music continued on, however.

"Niko, let's just go." Natalia's voice was strained.

Aldric hated that he couldn't see her. "Get away from her." His voice came out savage, more wolf than human. He needed to get to her, make sure she was okay. Why the hell was she here with some fucking vampire? And letting that male put his hands on her? He didn't care if he had no claim on her—the rational part of his brain was barely functioning.

Niko just tightened his jaw. "Let's go talk somewhere private."

Aldric's gaze darted to Natalia's delicate hand reaching around Niko, trying to gently tug him back.

The thin vestige of his control shredded. She shouldn't be touching this vampire, trying to protect him.

Mine, his wolf snarled as he lunged at Niko, using all his supernatural speed to close the twenty feet between them.

Vamps and shifters fell back around them like parting waves. Niko flashed his fangs as he leapt at Aldric, his own shorter claws visible as he raised a hand in attack.

Aldric readied for a blow as he prepared to mete out his own on this stupid, stupid male who thought he could touch what was his. Yep, the logical part of his brain had stopped functioning. Natalia wasn't his. But his wolf refused to admit it.

He was going for the male's throat. Any amount of pain he received in retaliation would be worth it if he could rip the male to pieces, to completely destroy him.

Midair, something large and heavy slammed into him from the side, sending him flying. Snarling, he turned on his attacker, only stopping a hair's breadth away from ripping at the male's throat. God, he hadn't even been paying attention to his surroundings, had only been focused on taking out that vampire.

Jayce stared down at him, pinning him to the floor. "Get your shit together." The words were low and full of authority, his expression black.

Aldric wanted to slash at him, destroy anyone who got in his way right now. But the visible scars on Jayce's face, put there by Aldric himself so long ago, stilled his instinct to fight. He'd made a lot of mistakes in his very long life. Attacking his brother again wouldn't be one of them. He had so many fucking regrets. The thought of hurting his brother again brought him off the ledge.

Barely.

"She's here." It was all he could manage to snarl out as he fought the struggle against his wolf, the need to shift forms. He wasn't sure why he was stating the obvious. He'd been suppressing all his thoughts about her for months, all his hunger where she was concerned. Seeing her in person had sliced through his control.

"You're acting like a savage." Jayce motioned behind him and Aldric knew that the vampire and Natalia were leaving, even though he couldn't see around his brother.

"I *am* a savage." Right now he felt more like one than he ever had. Just because they'd come out to humans didn't mean that supernaturals had shed the most primal part of themselves. He certainly hadn't.

"Not tonight you're not." Jayce's voice was calm even if his eyes were pure wolf.

Aldric needed to get his shit together. They were both here for the same reason. If he'd been thinking rationally earlier he'd have realized that the only reason Natalia was here was because she was working with Jayce. Aldric hadn't realized that Niko worked with Jayce but it made sense. He pushed out a harsh breath, his heart rate starting to even out, his desperate need to shift and attack receding. "Is she safe with him?" He needed to know. He might not be able to claim her for his own, but he still wanted her safe. Always.

A barely imperceptible nod.

That would have to do for now. The only thing he'd been able to focus on was that Niko had raked his teeth against Natalia's neck. That image was seared into his brain. When it threatened to make him go rabid again, Jayce shoved off him and pulled him to his feet.

Aldric rolled his shoulders, looking around and snarling at the partygoers. Natalia was definitely gone. Even if he couldn't see her, her scent was too faint for her to be here anymore. He shoved back all thoughts of her, forced himself to focus on his job. Because if he allowed himself to dwell on any part of her right now he'd throw away the last of his control and head out after her.

Vampires and shifters alike went back to talking and laughing now that the would-be fight was over before it had started. It wasn't exactly out of the ordinary for fights to break out at gatherings, not when different species were in attendance. But he didn't like bringing attention to himself, especially at an important function like this. Normally he was a ghost.

"We're going to talk later," he growled to his brother. Because it was fucked up that Jayce had brought Natalia into this without telling him.

"Nothing to talk about." Jayce tilted his chin, gesturing behind Aldric.

When Aldric turned he inwardly cringed. The Clifton coven leader and the Kinley pack Alpha were both heading toward them. He made eye contact with the Alpha, who just motioned for him to follow before turning on his heel and heading through the crowd.

Aldric was working for the Brethren and Jayce was working for The Council, which gave them both a sort of autonomy, but that didn't mean he went out of his way to start shit in someone else's home. It was poor form.

Because both those males were powerful. If they wanted to make his life difficult while he was investigating the disappearance of Arthur, they could stonewall him.

Jayce fell in step next to him. The crowd automatically parted for them as they headed after the two males. Aldric didn't have to ask where Kat was. If she wasn't with Jayce she must have left with Niko and Natalia.

The two males disappeared from sight behind an ornate door that was built into the wall. A vampire guard stepped back to let them through before closing the entrance behind them.

Aldric and Jayce were silent as they strode down a long hallway that was much darker than the ballroom they'd been in. Dim sconce lights lined the space, which ended at an open doorway.

Jayce stepped in first, Aldric right behind him, into a lavish sitting room.

"Shut the door behind you," Elian said quietly. Lean, almost slender, the vampire leader with dark brown skin was very strong and very old. Older than Aldric and Jayce—maybe even closer to a thousand, Aldric wasn't certain. Wearing a clearly custom-made tuxedo, he looked polished and elegant.

The polar opposite of shifter Alpha Craig Kinley, who was standing with his arms crossed over his massive chest next to a delicate-looking sitting chair. He was a bear of a man with skin darkened from the sun and covered in various scars. Unlike Elian, Craig had worn cargo pants, a T-shirt and had visible weaponry strapped to his body. Not that he'd need it in a fight. The male would simply go wolf. The weapons were more for show, Aldric guessed.

Elian's gaze landed on Aldric's, his amber eyes like shards of glass. "What was that out there?"

Before Aldric could answer, Jayce said, "Female problems."

He could have answered for himself, but the way Jayce spoke for him soothed something jagged inside him. He'd missed so many years with his brother because he'd been too afraid to look for him, too afraid of the rejection he thought he would face after what he'd done.

Craig snorted and Elian's mouth curved up ever so slightly as he nodded. "Okay." That one word dismissed the issue immediately. "We have a problem," he said, getting right to the point.

Aldric straightened. "You have news about Arthur?"

"No." Elian shook his head as Craig moved to a door opposite the one they'd come in through.

Craig opened the door to reveal a tall, slender female with auburn hair and tawny skin. The male's daughter, though Aldric had never met her in person. Dressed similarly to Craig, she stepped inside as the Alpha said, "Another one of Elian's vampires is missing. And not just any vampire."

"My mate," the female said. She cleared her throat, looked at her father. "Almost mate."

The Alpha nodded, his expression dark. "My daughter Constance was to mate with one of Elian's highest-ranked warriors—also Elian's nephew. Now he has disappeared as of last night."

Aldric frowned. A Kinley female was to be mated to a Clifton vampire? This was news to him. He looked at his brother. From Jayce's neutral expression he guessed he hadn't known about this would-be mating either. Arranged matings still happened, but he was surprised this particular female would agree to one. Or her father. The Alpha was fierce, and from what he knew of the male, he'd never sell her off, not even for peace.

As if he read his mind, Craig pinned Aldric with a sharp look. "They're in love. Have been hiding their relationship for some time." Annoyance vibrated through his words.

"When it became clear the two of them planned to mate, regardless of what we wished," the vampire leader interjected, giving Craig a wry look, "we decided it's time to officially end our feud. With a union like this, it will be a blood bond between our people. It's... time." He ran a hand over his face, the action very unlike the polished vampire Aldric had spoken with in the past. "With issues arising in this new world on a near-constant basis, we can't infight with each other anymore. It's not smart for business."

"My... Darius never would have left me or his coven. Something has happened to him," Constance said.

Her father nodded in agreement, even though his jaw was clenched tight. "She's correct. The vampire male would never abandon her."

Elian nodded as well.

"So *two* of your strongest people have disappeared in the last week?" Jayce looked between the two leaders.

Two solemn nods.

"Any leads on Darius?" Aldric asked. He was already investigating Arthur's disappearance and if these two disappearances were related, he'd be adding this to his job.

"Recent evidence has suddenly appeared, potentially linking me to Arthur's disappearance," Constance growled, rage infusing her words. "It's weak at best, but I found his blood in the back of my SUV. I went immediately to my father and Elian to tell them about it. I know Arthur so I recognized his scent. I'm not hiding this from you guys, but it's bullshit. So it could be that someone is trying to frame me for Arthur's disappearance, or at least throw suspicion on me, at the same time my mate is... kidnapped, or worse." Her voice broke on the last word.

Her father reached out, squeezed her shoulder once. It seemed to steady the female as she set her jaw and straightened.

Aldric looked at Jayce before he focused on the others. "Let's sit down and go over what you know." It was going to be a long night and while he wanted nothing more than to get to Natalia and talk to her without acting like a savage, this job was important.

If something ignited a war between these two powerful leaders, it would hurt both their species. And the fallout with the humans could be catastrophic.

Chapter 7

Natalia gave up the pretense of sleeping. It had been hours since she and Niko had returned to the shifter-run bed-and-breakfast. She still couldn't believe how violent Aldric had been.

On the bounty hunting missions she'd gone on with him, he'd always been so calm about everything. Even when others got violent against him, he'd been almost... Not exactly passive, but focused, intense. He'd bag his "prey," as he called the people he was hired to bring back, then be done with it.

Tonight he'd been a big jackass.

She slid out of bed, not bothering with the bedside light. She'd left her drapes open so moonlight bathed the room in pale beams. It wasn't a full moon, but it was close enough and the sight of it illuminating the darkness always calmed her lupine side.

Human myths about wolves needing to shift at a full moon or being forced to shift under one were just that—nonsense. Something most humans would know by now since shifters and vampires had come out to the world. But she still liked the moon, felt free running under it or even just looking at it. Something to do with her biology. When she was wolf things were simply better. Easier.

Kat had come back with her and Niko after Aldric's insane display, but Natalia didn't want to bother her friend right now. She slipped out into the hall, listened. All was quiet so she headed down the stairs, intending to make her way to the kitchen.

The owner of the B&B was a jaguar shifter and rented to supernatural beings only so there was no worry about any humans being around in case... Well, just in case something happened that human eyes didn't need to see. And record with their stupid freaking cell phones. They liked to put everything on social media.

As she reached the foyer she heard a faint rustling and peeked into the living room. Niko was sitting on a chaise longue, an e-reader in his hand.

"I would have thought you'd prefer paperback." She stepped into the room as he set it in his lap.

His smile was easy. "I can carry thousands of books at once. Humans hit the mark with this invention." There was a softness in his voice that surprised her.

"You like humans." She stepped farther into the room and perched on the edge of one of the tufted wingback chairs near him.

He nodded. "I do. Very much. They have such short, finite lives but some pack more into fifty years than I've seen my own kind do in hundreds. It's inspiring."

She felt the same, and for some reason was glad he did too. "You sound like my sister, Gloria."

"So, what brings you down here at one in the morning?"

"I could ask you the same thing."

"I'm waiting for Jayce."

Oh, right. She shrugged. "I can't sleep. I... don't know what was wrong with Aldric." For some reason she felt the need to apologize for him, to explain that he normally wasn't like that. It didn't make sense for him to go all caveman alpha.

Once upon a time they'd been friends. The male had even saved her life. She'd thought she might have a chance at more than just friendship with Aldric but he'd cut her out of his life. He'd left on a bounty hunting job that was only supposed to take a couple weeks at most.

That was over five months ago. Almost six now, if she wanted to get technical.

Since then he hadn't contacted her at all. And she knew he was alive and well thanks to his brother. Friends didn't just stop talking to each other for no reason, end a relationship like that. She'd already lost so many people in her life to murder that when he'd discarded her so easily it had cut viciously deep.

Niko snorted. "I know what was wrong with him. He wants to mate with you."

Once, that would have given her joy, thinking that he wanted to mate her. Now, not so much. Even if it was true, screw him. He'd lost his chance, betrayed their friendship.

Betrayed her.

She could never trust a male like that. "No, he doesn't." He'd made it clear he didn't even want to be friends with her. "He was with another female anyway." The sight of that beautiful female touching Aldric's arm was burned into her brain. Even remembering the way she'd touched him, as if she was familiar with him, made Natalia want to punch Aldric in the throat.

Niko's head tilted to the side just a fraction before the confusion fled his expression. "Ursula? He wasn't with her." The male scoffed. "Her mate is the one missing from the Clifton coven. Aldric's been hired by the Brethren to find him, just as we were hired by The Council."

She leaned back in the chair, tucking her legs under herself. "Did Jayce know he'd be there tonight?"

He snorted again. "Yep. That's why I'm waiting up. Fucker could've told me you two were involved," he grumbled. "I wouldn't have kissed your neck."

"We're *not* involved." After seeing him tonight she was more pissed than anything. She'd known he was okay because Kat would have told her otherwise, but seeing him in person, knowing he was fine and just living his life after cutting her out of his made her angry.

Niko eyed her as if he doubted her.

"I promise," she continued when he didn't respond. "We used to be friends. Now we're not." There was nothing more to say. Not to a stranger anyway.

He nodded once. "Okay."

She was under the impression he still didn't believe her but whatever. Before she could respond, the front door opened. Natalia scented Jayce as she turned. When she looked at the entryway and saw that it was only Jayce, she fought the stupid disappointment that Aldric wasn't with him.

She didn't want to see him anyway, she told herself. *Yeah, right.* She couldn't even swallow her own lie. "Is your brother okay?" she asked, even though she didn't want to talk about him. She still wanted to know that he wasn't in trouble or something. He'd tried to start a fight at a pretty big deal of a party.

Jayce nodded. "Yes. And... I'm sorry I didn't tell you two he would be there."

Niko made a grunting sound and stood. "That sounds like Kat forced you to apologize."

The enforcer lifted a shoulder, not denying it.

Natalia pushed up from her chair, wrapped her arms around herself. She didn't want to talk about Aldric more than necessary. "So what's the plan from here?"

"In a few hours we'll start listening to all the recordings from tonight, see if we hear anything useful. Vampires or shifters talking about anything to do with a kidnapped vampire seems too easy, but sometimes people talk when they've had too much to drink. Or when they think no one is listening. I've also got a few leads to start pulling on. Get some sleep though. Be down here by eight. We'll start fresh."

"I can be down earlier." She only needed five hours of sleep anyway, but could function on less if necessary.

He nodded once. "Then come down when you're ready to go. But get some sleep. I need everyone rested. The next couple days we're going to be hitting things hard. There's another vampire missing."

Natalia opened her mouth to ask more questions but Jayce shook his head. "Sleep. There's nothing you can do the next couple hours." He turned to Niko, basically dismissing her. "I have a task for you, however."

Instead of heading upstairs she went to the kitchen—and ate three peanut butter and honey sandwiches. Thankfully the owner of the B&B left the kitchen open to her guests, since they tended to have odd hours and big appetites. The food didn't do anything to quell her growing tension though.

Just when she thought she'd be able to put Aldric out of her mind he showed up on the mission she was on. This was supposed to have been something that was just hers. She didn't want him coming in and ruining it for her.

Annoyed, she washed her dish, then headed to her room. She couldn't avoid trying to sleep even if she wanted to. She needed rest if she was going to be sharp for whatever tomorrow—well, today—brought. But she had a feeling sleep would be elusive tonight.

When she reached the door, she frowned. Aldric's dark forest scent trickled out, oh so faintly.

She couldn't believe him, showing up like this after what he'd done. She didn't care what Niko had said—there was no way Aldric wanted to mate with her. And even if he did, he'd proven what kind of male he was. She couldn't trust him and didn't want him in her life.

Growling, she yanked her door open to find him sitting on the end of the bed—as if he had every right to be there.

Chapter 8

"What the hell are you doing in my room?" Natalia angrily whispered as she stepped into the bedroom, shutting the door quickly behind her.

She had on a long-sleeved pajama set with colorful bicycles on it, the top buttoned up, and Aldric wanted nothing more than to release each button slowly to reveal her to him. Then the image of Niko raking his teeth against the soft column of her neck popped into his mind and his wolf went a little crazy.

"You're not going to sleep with that fucking vampire!" The words were out before he could stop himself. He'd come here to talk calmly to her. Not start attacking. He inwardly winced. "Natalia—"

She blinked once, then that spitfire attitude he recognized well flared in her dark eyes as she cut him off. "I'll sleep with an entire coven if I want!" She wasn't whispering now. "You don't tell me what to do."

He covered the distance between them in the blink of an eye so they were toe to toe. He hadn't even realized he'd intended to move, but his wolf simply took over. For a moment, he inhaled, breathing her in as she looked up at him with a mix of emotions—hurt and anger being the two most prevalent. He hated that he was the cause of the hurt.

She didn't back down, something he adored about her. The first time they'd met on an elevator she'd told him to go fuck himself after he was rude to her—then she'd threatened to flay him alive when he pressed the emergency stop. Her temper always got him hot. Unlike any female he knew, she was... perfect. He should stay away from her. Rolling his shoulders once, he tried to ease back his growing tension. He couldn't get that image of Niko kissing her out of his brain.

"I'll kill any male who touches you." His voice was a low growl as he leaned down to get right in her face. Oh yeah, he was *not* making things better. But he couldn't seem to rein in his mouth. The thought of her with anyone but him made him rabid. It didn't seem to matter that he couldn't have her, that he didn't deserve her. His wolf wouldn't listen to reason.

Rolling her eyes, she shoved at his shoulder. "Get out of my room." Without waiting for a response, she sidestepped him and headed for her bed, starting to unbutton her top.

"What the hell are you doing?" he snarled. "We're still talking."

"Uh, you can talk all you want but I have nothing to say to you." She turned to face him, her expression defiant. Two buttons were undone, showing just a hint of creamy, smooth skin he'd been fantasizing about for too long. "And unless you plan to watch me get undressed, I'm going to bed." Her voice was a silky, challenging whisper.

His gaze strayed to the queen-sized bed for a moment. The comforter was frilly, this whole room filled with antiques. "I'm serious, you and that vamp—"

"Oh my God! Seriously, do you hear yourself? You cut yourself out of my life over five months ago. That was your choice." Rage vibrated in her voice as she stalked toward him. "You and I aren't even friends! And you think you can march back into my life and start giving me orders? Like what you think matters to me?" She shoved him in the middle of his chest. Hard.

He wanted to grab her hand, hold her close to him. But if he tried he was more likely to get clawed in the face. Deservedly so. He'd fucked up with her. Continually. Probably damaged their relationship in a way he could never repair. Pain splintered through his chest at the knowledge.

Her eyes were cold and bleak as she stared at him. "Get the hell out of my room or I will start shredding you."

"Damn it, Natalia, I'm sorry—"

"No. No apologies. I don't want to hear it. I don't want to hear your stupid voice. Months ago I would have, but you... God, Aldric. We were *friends*." For a brief moment her eyes glittered with unshed tears. She spun away from him, stalked to the open bathroom door. "Be gone when I come out."

His chest tightened at the waves of pain rolling off her. He wanted to go after her, to apologize but... words wouldn't mean shit. He thought he'd been doing the right thing by leaving her alone.

Bullshit, his wolf practically snarled.

Okay, he hadn't thought he'd been doing the right thing. She terrified him. What they could have together terrified him. The thought of losing her even more so. He couldn't survive that a second time. But the thought of losing her without even trying to win her over was even worse. The incident at the party made that crystal clear. He wasn't sure how he could win her over though. Not after the shit he'd pulled.

He was a fucking coward. Scrubbing a hand over his face he headed out the door instead of the window, which was the way he'd come in. He headed down to his brother and Kat's room, knocked once.

Kat opened the door, eyed him with pure annoyance. "You're an idiot."

He stepped inside as she let him pass. "Good to see you too," he muttered.

She snorted. "Dude, first that display at the party. Then you, what—break into her room and go all stupid alpha on her? I want to wring your neck right now."

Not bothering to respond, he went to the minibar in the corner of the room and made himself a drink. With his metabolism alcohol wouldn't do anything to him but he wanted the burn going down his throat. He threw back a shot of whiskey. "How'd you know I broke in?" he asked, turning around to face her. This place had incredible insulation. It was the way most supernatural establishments were built.

"Because I saw you scaling the tree outside earlier to get into her room. I'm just assuming that you went all alpha on her." She paused, her pale blue eyes narrowing. "At least tell me you didn't threaten to kill Niko."

He lifted a shoulder. "I threatened to kill *anyone* who touched her." While he felt shame at the way he'd left things between them months ago and the way he'd acted at the party, he wasn't sorry about threatening anyone who touched Natalia. He didn't know what that said about him. Maybe he really was still a savage.

"You and Jayce are definitely cut from the same cloth."

Jayce opened the bedroom door and nodded once at Aldric. His brother didn't seem surprised to see him.

"He broke into Natalia's room," Kat supplied before she greeted Jayce with a kiss.

"I know." Jayce's expression softened a fraction as he brushed his lips over Kat's.

Feeling as if he was intruding, Aldric looked away. He should just go to his room, but he'd wanted to talk to his brother first. Jayce had managed to get him a room here so he'd already brought his stuff over from the hotel he'd been staying at. Apparently The Council had paid for this place indefinitely so it was just them and the owner here. And unfortunately, Niko.

Stupid fucking vampire.

"Where's the vamp?" he asked, turning back to his brother as Jayce pulled away from Kat. Aldric knew Niko, though not as well as his brother. He didn't even want to say his name out loud right now. Even if he did like the guy. Or *had* liked the guy. After the way he'd touched Natalia at the party, he was close to hunting the male down and going wolf on him. Which yeah, was insane. His wolf wasn't listening to reason right now.

Kat snorted. "Could you sound any more disgusted? Niko's awesome. Don't get all mad because—" Abruptly stopping, she looked at Jayce.

They must be communicating telepathically as bonded mates could. A moment later Kat snorted, kissed her mate then looked at Aldric.

"I'll see you later. Gonna sneak in some food downstairs since I didn't get any at the party." She gave him a pointed look before heading out of the room. "Be gone by the time I get back."

Despite his mood he laughed at the teasing note in her voice. He understood she wanted time alone with her mate. Even though he was so lonely he ached with it, the happiness he felt for his brother eclipsed any sadness. If there was a greater power in the universe, he was certain that Kat and Jayce had been created for each other.

"She's going to set the alarm too now that we're all in. In case you were wondering." Jayce unhooked his sheathed blades and laid them on a settee near the window.

Aldric had planned to sit outside Natalia's room, considering what he'd thought was a lack of security here.

"I've set up extra security precautions as well. And the owner was aware of you entering Natalia's room. She sent me a message, wanted to know if she should contain you."

He raised his eyebrows at that. Good to know they actually had security. He hadn't seen cameras but they must be out there. He hadn't met the owner yet, wasn't sure who she was or how powerful she was. To run a supernatural establishment like this on her own, she'd have to be able to take care of herself though. That was certain. Some of the tension humming through him eased. "So, Niko—"

"Is working with me. And you will be civil to him. He feels no animosity toward you after tonight. You know what he's like."

Aldric just grunted. The truth was Niko was one of the most decent vamps he'd ever met. Good-natured, the male had more than retained his humanity. Aldric might not admit it out loud, but he felt like shit for the way he'd attacked him.

Jayce gave him a pointed look. "You need to get your shit together where Natalia is concerned."

His instinct was to buck the command in his brother's voice. His wolf didn't like to take orders from anyone. It was why he worked so well alone or in charge of a group. "I am under control."

Jayce watched him with cool gray eyes. "Are you?"

He paused. "I will be."

"You fucked up with her. Something you already know."

His chest tightened at his brother's words. He didn't need the truth rubbed in his face. Or maybe he did.

"The only thing I need to know right now is can you work with her knowing that she might hate you, that she might never forgive you, only tolerate you?"

He nodded once, his jaw tight. "I can. I will." He'd hurt Natalia, knew he might not be able to undo the damage regardless of what he wanted at this point. The choice to be friends or more was solely up to her. Knowing he might not ever get even her friendship gutted him.

But he *had* to try. Their relationship had been one of the bright spots in his miserable life. He wanted a hell of a lot more than friendship but he'd have to start there, to rebuild what he'd broken. He scrubbed a hand over his face. "I don't know what the fuck is wrong with me," he rasped out, the admission hard. He never should have cut and run the way he had. He'd let his cowardice take over.

Jayce's expression didn't change, but his eyes went human again. "You've got to let go of the past."

He didn't respond to that, couldn't. It brought up too much shit he didn't want to deal with. "What's your strategy after tonight?" Changing the subject was the only thing he could do now. Getting into hunting mode, finding who'd taken Arthur and the other vamp male, would keep him focused.

"I'm going to start listening to the feeds collected from tonight. I've sent Niko to scout a club we'll be hitting in"—he glanced at his watch—"seventeen hours."

"A vamp club?"

"Yeah. He'll be able to get in a few hours this morning before sunrise, see if he can learn anything on his own. He'll be able to blend in better since he's a vamp." Aldric nodded as Jayce continued. "We'll be there close to the next opening."

Which would be right around sunset. "Is this Club Inferno?"

His brother lifted an eyebrow. "Yes."

"I'd planned to go there too. Got a tip that Arthur was last seen there."

"What did his mate say about that?"

"She doesn't know." And Aldric didn't plan to tell her that her mate had gone to a sex club without her. Some vampires might have open relationships but Arthur and Ursula didn't. He'd received a text from one of his contacts on his way to the B&B tonight who was certain that Arthur had been there the other night. It was a solid lead he couldn't ignore. "How'd you find out he was there?"

In typical Jayce form, he didn't answer. "Want to help me sift through all these recordings tonight?"

"Yeah." Because he wouldn't be sleeping anytime soon. "Will Kat mind?"

"Nah. Kat knows what it's like on an investigation. We can take this downstairs so she can get a few hours' rest." Again, Jayce's expression changed ever so slightly when he said Kat's name.

Aldric cleared his throat, tried to keep his voice casual. "Natalia going to the club tomorrow?"

"She'll be going in with Niko. They work well together." Jayce reached for a couple laptops, which would likely be their work stations. Before Aldric could respond, Jayce continued. "If you can handle yourself, the three of you can go in as a threesome."

"Okay." And he would keep his emotions in check. There was no excuse for his behavior tonight, but now that he knew for a fact that Natalia and Niko weren't together, he could force his primal nature to behave.

He hoped.

Chapter 9

Arthur kept his eyes closed and his breathing even when he heard the scraping sounds. So far, he knew he was in a silver-lined cage in a dungeon of sorts.

And completely naked.

Whoever had constructed his prison knew how to contain vampires.

But people always made mistakes. When the time was right, he would escape. Or die trying.

He wasn't sure how long he'd been here or who had taken him. Other than that one female voice he remembered hearing before going unconscious in the woods, he hadn't heard anyone speak again.

He'd woken up in the cage with a mattress and pillow. Nothing else. He'd received a couple small bags of blood, but hadn't drunk them. He'd scented drugs in them so he'd emptied them under his mattress, letting the mattress soak up the liquid. Not the best plan but there was nowhere else to dispose of the blood.

He'd thought someone might come into the cage to retrieve the empty bags, giving him a chance to attack, but so far no one had.

Now, he heard something new. A metallic, dragging sound. Like...the sound of chains along a concrete floor. And groaning.

He slowly opened his eyes and tilted his head to the side. He had visibility of two other cages next to his and a brick wall in front of them. Dim track lighting lined the low ceiling over the wall but he didn't need it to see. Not with his vampiric senses.

A hooded figure with gloved hands was dragging a groaning male along the floor. Even with the hood, Arthur could see the tall individual was female. It was in the lithe way she moved.

When she opened the cage next to his, the male kicked out, slamming his booted foot against her knee.

She cried out in surprise, but moving lightning quick with the speed only a supernatural creature possessed, she brought a weapon up and shot two darts into the male, who quickly slumped to the floor.

Arthur's blood chilled as he recognized the male. Darius Clifton. Elian's nephew.

After that the female unhooked his chains, and stripped him naked, neatly wrapping his clothing up and tucking it under her arm. Then she patted his face almost...adoringly. Arthur filed that away. Something tickled his nose. Another scent, a familiar one. He couldn't place it though. It was in the recesses of his mind but he couldn't make the connection.

As if the female sensed him watching, she looked over and he saw only a gold mask beneath the hood, covering her entire face. He couldn't even see the color of her skin because of the turtleneck visible under the hood.

She could be wearing a mask because she planned to let them go and didn't want to be recognizable. Or more likely she was wearing one in case they escaped. They wouldn't be able to identify her.

There were always other ways to identify someone though. Unfortunately she wasn't a big talker. Now that he wasn't drugged he hoped she said something again.

Instead she raised her weapon and fired at him through the bars.

Moving on instinct, he rolled off the flimsy mattress, easily dodging the dart that flew past him.

She shot again and again. Left, right, he dodged as more darts tore through the air. At one point he jumped high in the air, using his claws to attach to the ceiling.

Just as quickly he let go, as the silver coating started to burn his skin. Ignoring the pain, he twisted in midair as another dart would have hit him.

Letting out a sound of frustration she let her weapon hand fall to her side. She stared at him for a few long moments. Picking up the chains in her gloved hands she turned on her heel. With the exception of the rattling chains, her movements were whisper quiet.

Tense, he waited for her to return. As he did, he scanned the cage once again. His neighbor wasn't waking up any time soon so he couldn't ask him if he knew who'd taken them and why.

He thought about trying to escape through the floor. The concrete floor wasn't lined in silver but it could be rigged with explosives or sensors.

Deciding to wait until Darius regained consciousness so they could devise a plan, and to find out what Darius knew of their kidnapper, he lay back on his mattress and conserved his strength. He could go a long time without fresh blood but it would still drain his energy reserves.

Resting now was the smartest thing. He might be old, strong and hard to kill, but he was in a fucking cage right now. He had to get out, get back to his mate. He'd been forcing back thoughts of her as much as he could so emotion wouldn't cloud his mind. He needed to focus on getting out.

And discovering who the hell was stupid enough to take him in the first place.

Chapter 10

Aldric stared at the ceiling, knowing sleep was a joke. After listening to those audios and watching some of the recordings, he and Jayce had made notes of various people to follow up with. Then they'd had to get some downtime in order to function the rest of the day.

But right now, all he could think about was Natalia. It didn't matter that he should be focused on the investigation.

She consumed him. When he closed his eyes, the night they first met replayed over in his mind. He hadn't learned her name that night, but her scent had been embedded in his brain.

Arms crossed over his chest, Aldric stood in front of the vintage elevator, waiting for the fucking thing to open so he could get upstairs into the supernatural club and take care of business. He just wanted to do his job and get out tonight. He glanced over as a petite female headed his way.

Dark hair, dark eyes and...sexy. He looked away quickly, dismissing her. For the first time in centuries his wolf woke up. He wanted to lean over and drag in the stranger's scent.

She didn't stand too close to him, but a subtle cherry blossom and vanilla scent teased the air, making him edgy—hungry. She was also watching him intently. Though he noted that she was careful to stay out of his personal space. Still, he didn't like being on the receiving end of such intensity.

When he clenched his jaw, she immediately snapped her gaze forward. The elevator halted on the bottom floor. The doors opened to reveal a sleek, modern interior despite the vintage exterior.

The female's boots clicked on the flooring as they entered together. And he noticed that she was watching him again.

"You look... Have we met before? Did you go to Duke?" Her voice was soft, sultry.

He snorted, realizing she was hitting on him, and glanced at her. He preferred to be the pursuer and he never went after someone who looked as fucking innocent as her. She even smelled innocent. "Not interested," he muttered.

Her big eyes widened even more. Then to his surprise, she laughed right in his face. "Go fuck yourself. I wasn't hitting on you. You just look like my friend's mate, Jayce, but... okay then, whatever." Rolling her eyes, she turned to face the doors.

At the sound of his estranged brother's name, his entire body jolted. He turned to her again as she pulled out a cell phone and started texting.

On instinct he pressed the emergency stop. He needed to know if this female knew his brother.

She glared at him. "What's the matter with you?"

"Did you say Jayce?"

"I swear to God, if you don't release that button I'm going to flay you alive." Temper flared in her dark gaze, her body language edgy, as if she was ready to attack him right then and there.

To his surprise, he felt a smile tugging at his lips. "You're quick-tempered for such a little thing." Even in her heeled boots she was barely five feet, five inches.

Her canines and claws descended. "You want to find out what this little thing can do?"

For some reason, the sight of her all worked up got him hot. That alone disturbed him, should have been enough to tell him to back the fuck off. He hadn't let his guard down with a female in centuries, didn't want a female in his life. Not after he'd spectacularly failed his mate. Realizing he might be frightening the female, he let the button go. "Were you referring to Jayce Kazan a moment ago?" He kept his voice civilized, polite.

She sniffed haughtily in a way that had his cock coming to full attention. "So what if I was?" Turning from him, she shoved her phone back in her pocket, clearly ignoring him as she watched the numbers move by on the elevator.

"He's mated?" The news nearly knocked him on his ass. His brother, who he

hadn't seen in centuries, was mated? God knew Jayce deserved the happiness. Aldric scrubbed a hand over his face. He wished he could get over his fear, the terror of reaching out to his brother.

The female lifted a shoulder as the elevator stopped on level nine. The music from the club pulsed around them as the doors whooshed open.

"So what are you doing here by yourself, little wolf?" He tried to keep his voice steady, deciding to take a different approach. He'd been rude to her and needed to remedy that if he was going to learn anything about Jayce. The truth was, he didn't like the thought of this female here by herself. She should have packmates watching out for her.

Too many things inundated him at once: the music, scents and so many damn voices. Aldric rolled his shoulders. This place was supposed to be owned by some-one supernatural. Normally supernatural-owned places kept the music at a lower decibel because of shifter and vamp hearing. The noise grated against him but he ignored it, focused on the female.

"I'm not by myself." Again with the haughty sniff as she strode toward the entrance where a security guy stood next to a roped-off entryway.

Yeah, his wolf wanted her and wanted her bad. He felt as if he could crawl out of his skin as he kept pace with her.

The vampire bouncer subtly scented them instead of carding them, then lifted a heavy, velvet rope to let them pass.

"Let me buy you a drink." He needed to know if this female truly knew Jayce, and okay, he wanted to talk to her. Find out her name.

"No, thank you." She glanced away from him, clearly looking for someone.

This part of the club was on three levels. The first floor had three bars and a dance floor, which she was currently scanning. Looking for a boyfriend maybe? He nearly snarled at the thought, but caught himself.

What the fuck was wrong with him?

High-top tables surrounded three sides of the dance floor, and the second floor—which was actually the tenth floor of the building—had reserved areas. Curtains were pulled back on the empty booths that reminded him of opera boxes, while others were hidden for privacy.

Flashing strobe lights flicked around the place, giving him a headache. "Listen, I just... do you seriously know Jayce Kazan?"

She looked at him again, her expression filled with mistrust as she shrugged. "Kind of. I met him a while ago. It's not like we hang out or anything. What's your deal? And what's your name?"

She was lying, he was certain of it. He stared at her for a long moment. The female hadn't actually answered his question, had more or less evaded in answering. "My name's Aldric." He watched her, waiting to see if there was a spark of recognition in those dark, beautiful eyes.

She raised her eyebrows, clearly not impressed.

Stepping back, he nodded once at her. "I'm sorry I bothered you. Enjoy your evening." Before she could respond he blended back into the crowd.

He wasn't sorry he'd met her, not one little bit. Deep down, in a place he didn't want to admit existed, he was certain he'd see the female again. It disturbed him on the most primal level that he actually wanted to see her. But he would make it happen.

Chapter 11

Beyond frustrated, Natalia punched her pillow and got out of bed. The bed and breakfast had incredible insulation but some things couldn't be masked. She didn't hear anything but there was a subtle scent of mating in the air.

Someone, and she didn't have to guess who, was having sex right now. It was making her wolf even edgier because the one male she wanted was under the same roof. Not that it mattered.

She was so angry at him, and concerned about the mission. She desperately wanted to be an asset, to prove that she could help. Now his presence threatened to ruin what she'd been trying to do. Those two missing vampires needed help. Not only that, they had to stop the Kinley pack and Clifton coven from starting a war and putting all other supernaturals in danger. Including her own pack. Her sisters and cousins had been through enough in the last year. She wouldn't let anything else happen because of a bunch of supernaturals who couldn't get their shit together.

Gah, why did Aldric have to be here at all? After that ridiculous display at the party she knew he had to be somewhat attracted to her. But it didn't matter. That was just biology. He wanted her. So what?

It was too early to be awake but she wasn't going to be able to sleep so she took a quick shower and changed into jeans and a dark blue cashmere sweater. She'd gone running in wolf form earlier and it hadn't helped get rid of her frustration. She couldn't stay cooped up in her room any longer. As she made her way downstairs in search of food, the sweet aroma of coffee trickled up.

Inhaling deeply, she picked up her pace. The swinging door to the kitchen was propped open and she could see Niko inside, pouring a mug at one of the beige granite countertops. "I didn't know vamps drank coffee."

"I got hooked on Starbucks when they first came out. Can't get enough."

"I can't tell if you're kidding."

Sliding an empty mug to her as she approached, he lifted an eyebrow. "Sadly, I am not."

Laughing lightly, she poured herself a mug. "When did you get back?" She'd seen him heading out on his motorcycle a few hours ago when she'd been out running in wolf form, trying to expend some energy.

"Ten minutes ago."

They still had an hour or so until sunrise. "So?"

"So what?" He took a sip of his coffee.

"What's the club like? Is it super kinky?" She'd never been to a sex club before. Had never wanted to. But just because she was a virgin didn't mean she wasn't curious.

He lifted a dismissive shoulder. "Like all the other ones."

She blinked, though she wasn't sure why she was surprised. He was hundreds of years old and a vampire. Of course he would have been to a sex club before. "Oh."

"You'll get to see firsthand later tonight. But I can say this one was... Classier is the wrong word, but it's lusher than some others I've seen."

"Do you go to them often?"

"No. Just when I'm working."

"What exactly do you do for a living anyway?" Niko worked with Jayce on occasion but she knew he didn't need to. Kat had mentioned that the male felt he owed Jayce—a debt for saving his life once—but had more money than some small countries.

He gave her a wicked grin. "Lots of things."

It was clear he didn't plan to expand on that so she rolled her eyes. "Fine, be that way..." She trailed off as Aldric's scent filled the air.

Her gut tightened even as her wolf pushed to the surface, eager to get closer to the male. Annoyingly traitorous bitch. She hated that her wolf wanted to run around and preen for this male when she should just punch him in the face.

A moment later he appeared in the entryway of the kitchen, his body stiff.

Niko cleared his throat, nodded once at Aldric before he leaned over and kissed Natalia on the forehead. "I'm gonna enjoy my coffee outside." Then he was gone before she could blink, shutting the door to the back porch behind him in a soundless whisper.

When she looked at Aldric his jaw was clenched tight and his eyes were pure lupine. At least he hadn't attacked Niko, but he could get the hell over himself already. Even though she'd planned to make some really early breakfast, coffee would have to be enough for now. Maybe she'd go for another run, burn off all her excess energy. It would be a long run.

Not bothering to give the male even a tight smile, she started to leave but he held up his hands briefly. "Can we talk? No threats from me, I promise."

Part of her wanted to simply leave but she was too curious about what he had to say. "Fine, talk."

"I'm sorry about the way I reacted last night at the party."

"And this morning in my room?"

Jaw tight, he nodded. "Yes. I lost control. My behavior was unacceptable."

"Huh. We agree on *something*."

He rubbed a hand over his face. "I'm also sorry for my disappearing act the last five months. I…" He cleared his throat.

A small part of her ached to reach out and comfort him because it was clear he was struggling. But that was just stupid. She hated that he affected her like that, made her care for him after the way he'd ghosted, as if she meant nothing to him. She didn't have many friends. Her pack was tightly-knit, and even though she'd gone to college and had some human friends she still kept in contact with, her pack were her people, her inner circle.

She'd let Aldric into that circle and he'd thrown her friendship back in her face. Which pissed her off beyond belief. There might be chemistry between them, but that would never erase the fracture between them, what he'd done.

The back door opened and Niko stuck his head in at the same time Felicity, the proprietor, entered through the swinging door.

"Ursula's here to speak to you," Niko said to Aldric.

The petite jaguar shifter who ran the B&B scanned the three of them, her expression neutral. "Visitors are allowed, but I need to be informed how many and a general time frame of their arrival, for security reasons. I need to be able to keep my guests safe. I knew about you," she said to Aldric, "from your brother. Feel free to use doors from now on."

Natalia snickered. She wasn't sure how old the jaguar shifter was. It was difficult to tell with supernaturals, but the dark-haired female looked to be in her thirties by human standards.

"I take it the vampire out front is a friend, not a foe?" she asked.

Aldric nodded. "Yes. Apologies. From now on any visitors will be announced." He gave Natalia a frustrated look before ducking outside.

Natalia should be grateful he'd left. It spared her from having to talk to him any longer. Even if she did want to hear what he had to say. Like, maybe the reason why he'd disappeared on her. One that made sense. Not excuses. Because if he gave her excuses, it would be even worse than whatever the truth was.

At least with him gone Natalia could breathe normally again. And that raw energy humming through her at the mere sight of him had started to recede. He just got her so damn wound up.

"Does anyone need anything right now?" Felicity's dark hair was pulled into a loose bun at her nape and she wore jeans and a flowy red sweater-tunic.

Niko shook his head. "I've already fed, but thank you."

"I'm okay too," Natalia said. "I'll probably just grab some muffins. They smell delicious." There was a big basket of them, and a few of them would hit the spot. "Sorry if we woke you up."

Felicity's smile was kind. "I keep odd hours, it's fine, trust me."

As Felicity left Natalia grabbed the basket of muffins. She'd return it to the kitchen later. Since she couldn't sleep, she could help out by listening to the recordings for a few hours before Jayce and Kat came down. She figured Jayce had already listened to them for a while anyway. The male never seemed to sleep.

Niko raised his eyebrows. "You planning on eating the whole basket?"

"Probably. Hey, I'm going to check out the recordings. Jayce told me earlier what I needed to listen and look for. You want to join me or are you about to head to bed?"

"I'll help for a couple hours."

"Great." She'd have to give all her attention to the recordings so she didn't miss anything, but she was glad for the company, even if they wouldn't be talking.

As they left the kitchen, she tried not to think about the male outside or what he was doing. He wasn't her business.

If only she could truly convince herself of that.

Chapter 12

Aldric tried to tamp down his annoyance as he stepped outside. He'd wanted to apologize to Natalia, even if it was just the beginning of making things right to her. Deep down, he wasn't sure he ever could. She'd looked at him so coldly, as if he meant nothing to her.

Rounding the back of the house, he headed for the front yard. The bed and breakfast was on a quiet street on the outskirts of the downtown area. Some of the neighbors were shifters, according to Jayce, but many were human.

Why the hell was Ursula here?

Instead of the dress she'd had on earlier, she wore pants, boots and a thick coat over a turtleneck. Everything was black except for her gold earrings. Her arms were crossed over her chest as he reached her. "You haven't been returning my calls."

"I texted you."

Her gold-amber eyes flashed bright. "Not good enough. I need updates," she snapped, the command in her tone something his wolf didn't like.

Aldric forced himself to remain calm. This was a female who was worried about her mate. He could respect that. "I was busy following up on leads. Texting you was all I could do." He wouldn't give her specifics. Even if he didn't think she'd had anything to do with her mate's disappearance, it didn't mean someone in her life wasn't involved. "And the more time I spend with you is time I spend away from doing my job."

She swallowed hard, her expression crumpling. "I... It's almost time for me to go to sleep and I hate sleeping while he's out there maybe hurt or worse. I feel like I should be doing more."

Ah, fuck. "I know." He softened his voice. "The waiting isn't going to get easier but you've *got* to let me do my job. I have a one hundred percent success rate of finding people." Usually targets, individuals he considered prey. And not always alive. But he was good at what he did. "You've already done a lot," he added, wanting to soothe her a little. The pain on her face was real. "You've given me access to all his phone and credit card records, and given me a list of all his enemies." He could have gotten most of it on his own and had still followed up to be sure she'd given him everything, but her help had made his job easier.

She wrapped her arms around herself, shivered, even though he knew she wasn't cold. "I'll stop bothering you. And thank you."

When she turned to leave, he spoke again. "Is Arthur close to Darius Clifton?" He already knew the answer, but he wanted to gauge her response.

She nodded. "Yes, very. We often socialize with him." Something flashed in her eyes, something he couldn't even begin to define.

"Have they ever had a falling out?"

"Not that I know of." *Definite truth there.*

"What was it you thought of before, when I first mentioned Darius's name."

She bit her bottom lip, tension vibrating off her. "Is Darius involved in Arthur's disappearance?" Disbelief laced her words.

"I won't rule anything out, but no, I don't believe so."

"Is what I tell you confidential?"

"For the most part, yes."

Sighing, she said, "Darius is involved with the Kinley Alpha's daughter. And I mean seriously *involved*. They want to get mated. The only reason they've held off is out of respect for her father and his uncle. I... don't think they'll hold off much longer though."

He nodded.

She blinked. "You already know this?"

"Yes." No need to tell her it was a recent discovery or that Darius was missing. That wasn't up to him to reveal.

"We've had the two of them over on multiple occasions and gone to various functions together. Constance and I... We have different interests but she's a lovely young lady. For a…"

"For a shifter?" he asked wryly. Clearly she'd forgotten who she was talking to. Ursula shrugged. "Sorry."

"What kind of functions? I was under the impression that their relationship wasn't common knowledge."

"It's not. And we used Elian's jet to get away, usually to the city for a play or the ballet. We also took some occasional trips to Chicago."

"This is good. Can you make a list of every place you went with them? And a list of every single person who knows about their relationship." He and Jayce had already gathered the latter list from Constance but Ursula might know more. "Does your staff know?"

"I will, and no, they don't."

"Okay, thank you. Can you send it tonight?"

"As soon as I return home I'll get to work on the list. Why do you want to know about Darius's connection with Arthur?"

"I can't tell you right now. But as soon as I'm able, I will. Do *not* tell anyone about this."

"I won't. And thank you for not brushing me off."

"I swear I'll do everything I can to get him back."

Jaw set, she simply nodded and turned away, moving across the yard in the blink of an eye.

When Aldric stepped back into the kitchen, he locked the door behind him. Of course Natalia wasn't there anymore, even if the subtle traces of her scent were. The cherry blossom and vanilla aroma was now embedded in his psyche.

He hated the interruption they'd had, but at least he'd come up with a potential lead. Or he would, once Ursula got that list to him. Constance had mentioned that they socialized with Arthur but he might be able to get more from Ursula. Ursula would have a better pulse on the Clifton coven, would know who was privy to the secret of the vampire-shifter relationship.

As he headed down the hallway toward the front of the house he followed Natalia's scent instead of going up to his room. In the living room, headphones on, she sat with her back to him on one of the cream-colored couches. Niko was next to her and also had headphones on as they listened to recordings on Jayce's computers.

They were aware of him. He could see it in their body language. Niko half-turned, nodded at him, but she didn't turn at all.

Only the back of her head was visible above the back of the couch, but a mirror hung on the blue-and-cream-striped wall opposite her. Her eyes were on the laptop screen and her shoulders went stiff at his presence.

Even though he wanted to stay, to be around her, he didn't want to make her uncomfortable. She didn't deserve that.

Right now wasn't about his own needs. He'd fucked up and needed to make things right. If he even could.

Sighing, he picked up his own laptop. He'd finish listening to the recordings he had in his room, then try to grab a few hours of sleep.

They might be heading to the vampire club at sunset but he had other leads he could follow up on before then. Months ago he would have asked Natalia to go with him.

He wondered if he asked her later if she'd consider going with him. More likely she'd just laugh in his face.

And he would deserve it.

Chapter 13

"We'll see you guys in a few hours." Jayce took Kat's hand as they slid out of the SUV and stepped onto the sidewalk.

Aldric nodded from the backseat where he'd sat next to them. Niko nodded from the driver's seat.

Natalia smiled at them from the passenger seat. "Be safe."

Jayce resisted the urge to snort as Kat said, "We will." He was the fucking enforcer and over five hundred years old. No one had truly cared about what happened to him for so long. Not even The Council. At least not cared about him in the sense his new pack did.

Even if he wanted to deny it, even if he'd flat-out told Connor Armstrong he'd never be his Alpha, Jayce still thought of the Armstrong-Cordona pack as his people. So many of the females had this habit of worrying about him and Kat when they were gone. It was... nice. Though he'd never admit that shit out loud to anyone.

"If I was still human, I'd never walk in this neighborhood alone at night. It's creepy." Kat glanced around what had once been a bustling area of town as the SUV pulled away, headed in the other direction. Only four blocks down the road was a strip of successful human nightclubs. And during the day that same area had open cafes, shops and businesses.

But a little farther south, part of the neighborhood had been eaten away. Jayce had seen it happen over the centuries all over the world. This four-block strip of nothing was more of a barrier between a "good" part of town and a less-than-savory one.

A vampire owned all the property along this area, including a club right in the middle of the four-block radius that was supernaturals only. Jayce knew the owner, and while he didn't like the guy, he could respect that rule. There were some things humans didn't need to be part of. Not when they were so much more breakable than the other species.

"I'll keep you safe if you're scared," he murmured teasingly, pulling his delectable mate closer.

She'd dressed in the most ridiculous outfit tonight and it was still hot as fuck on her. The plaid red and black Band-Aid-sized skirt barely covered her ass, the hem an inch higher than her black thigh-high boots. Even though it was freezing out she had on a bright pink faux fur crop top that showed off her flat, lean stomach. Her neon purple wig was a sleek, shiny bob, highlighting her sharp cheekbones. She'd never been to a sex club before and told him this was how she envisioned people dressed there. She wasn't that far off the mark.

While the most possessive part of him hated that others would be able to see her dressed like this, his wolf was completely secure that this female wanted no other but him.

She started to say something when he sensed another presence. Not Aldric, Niko or Natalia. They were parking a mile away and would be joining them in an hour. He would recognize their scents anyway.

Dropping Kat's hand, he pulled out his blades in milliseconds, the move automatic. His blades had been blessed by the fae before he'd been born and were nearly indestructible. If he killed a supernatural being with one, that individual would disintegrate into dust. And, as Kat had learned not so long ago, if he killed humans taking vampire blood with them, those humans would also turn to dust. His blades had a very specific purpose.

Kat's claws were out by the time he'd drawn both weapons and turned on the sidewalk to face whoever was moving up on them far too quietly for his taste. His wolf clawed to the surface, the need to protect his mate a live thing inside him.

These two had made a stupid mistake by trying to sneak up on them. Both vampires, if he scented correctly. Jayce's gaze swept over them, taking in everything in milliseconds. Their aggressive stance, their clothing and the weapon each held.

Guns.

His wolf sneered at the guns. One of the vamps started to raise his weapon. Jayce lunged, using all his supernatural speed. He slashed out at the male's arm, cutting it off in one smooth stroke as he stabbed the other one in the upper shoulder, piercing all the way through.

Both males screamed. He kicked the one on the right in the stomach, sending the male flying back ten feet as he held his free blade to the throat of the male who had a sword impaled through his shoulder.

"You want to die tonight?" he growled.

No longer screaming, the male was breathing hard as he shook his head. Jayce knew what he was thinking, could see it in the way his hand twitched.

"Don't even think about it." Jayce could see the outline of another gun under the guy's thick down jacket. "You go for it, I'll cut your head off." These males were young. That much was clear in not only their scent but in their pathetic moves. They hadn't even been able to sneak up on him properly, let alone attack.

Weak. His wolf sneered again, insulted these two fuckers thought they could attack him and his mate.

The one on the ground remained where he was, cradling his bloody stump as his breath sawed in and out erratically. Just because they were supernatural didn't mean they didn't feel pain.

"Take out your wallets. Slowly. Then toss them to her." He didn't bother motioning to Kat nor sheathing his blades. He might be old and well-trained, but he wasn't going to get cocky and take his eyes off a threat. Not when his mate was in the vicinity.

"Wait, what?" The one with the blade against his neck swallowed hard. "You robbing us?"

"That's what you planned to do to us, right?" They probably robbed humans unfortunate enough to be on this desolate strip.

Without responding, the male slowly pulled out his wallet as the male on the ground did the same.

"Face down on the sidewalk," Jayce ordered, stepping back. "Both of you."

Once they were lying down, he removed all of their weapons—all six of them, including knives. Then he wiped off his bloody blades on their clothes. "I'm going to find out who your maker is. If he doesn't deal with you, I'll kill all of you.

The rancid stench of fear that rolled off them was more potent than when he'd cut off the male's hand. Which told Jayce their maker didn't know what they were up to.

"Now run," he growled softly. "If I see you again tonight, I'll fucking kill you."

Bleeding profusely, the males stumbled to their feet and took off moving as fast as they could while wounded. The severed limb would eventually grow back, but the guy grabbed his arm anyway.

"That was actually kind of nice. For you." Kat sounded surprised as he turned to her.

He sheathed his blades, bundled up the confiscated weapons and took her hand again as he lifted a shoulder. He should have killed them for simply daring to threaten his mate but...he hadn't wanted to do it in front of her. Even if he knew she could handle it. Didn't mean he wanted her to see death more than she had to. "Not worth my time. Besides, their maker is going to take care of them."

She shuddered slightly. "Ugh, I hope so. God, their fear was nauseating. So how are you sure this club owner is even here?"

"A source informed me Ferguson never left the country. It lines up with what I've discovered tracking his movements." The owner of Club Inferno was difficult to locate, however. So just because Jayce couldn't pinpoint his exact location at any given time wasn't strange. The fact that Ferguson had been avoiding Jayce's attempts to contact him, however, was.

They weren't remotely friends, but the older male had never given Jayce grief before when he'd been working an investigation. And there weren't that many supernatural-only sex clubs in North America, so the male's establishment was often a hot spot for certain clientele.

"Even if he's not here, I'll still be collecting all of their video surveillance for the last couple weeks." Or someone was going to die.

Kat shot him a sideways look, her pale blue eyes darkening with a need that he recognized well. "I love it when you use that 'fuck with me and die' voice."

All his muscles tightened at the sharp scent of lust that rolled off her. He had to lock down his reaction to her, force his body under control. He still wasn't sure what he'd done to deserve her, but he'd fucking die for her. He just wished his brother would get his shit together because he was certain the male could find real happiness with Natalia.

As they approached what looked like a run-down four-story apartment complex, he slowed.

"Seriously, *this* is it?" Kat's voice was full of disbelief as she eyed the place. Graffiti covered most of it, crude and obnoxious phrases, as well as busted-out windows.

"It's an illusion."

She blinked. "What?"

"What you're seeing isn't really what's here. It's a very weak one and if something were to disrupt it, it would fall away to reveal a modern three-story warehouse-style building in pristine condition."

Her eyes widened. "Can you see it?"

"No, but I can see the glimmer of it." It was as if there was a faint sheet draped over it, rippling slightly under the moon and city lights. "I've seen it fall before, however."

"That's...weird." She frowned. "Of all people, I should be able to see it, right?"

His mate was a seer, had been one as a human, and that gift transferred when she'd been turned into a shifter. She could often see below an individual's true self, could see the vampire's bloodlust or fangs, or a shifter's animal lurking beneath the surface. She'd known about the supernatural world before they'd actually come out to humans. But some things even he didn't understand. "I don't know."

Is this like a vampire power, like the one Niko has? she asked telepathically, using their mating link.

No... Well, yes, some vampires have that ability, but Ferguson doesn't. Maybe because it's created from magic you can't see it. Or maybe because it's an inanimate object, not a sentient being. Whatever the reason, it wasn't important. Jayce tilted his head to where he knew a video camera was, even if he couldn't see it. He let his wolf show in his gaze before he tugged Kat up a set of four stairs.

Once they moved up the stairs, the illusion faded to reveal the sleek building and a frosted glass and chrome door. The glass was thick and bullet resistant. A blurred figure stood behind the door to the right.

A moment later it opened. A vampire male dressed in a black suit and a cherry-red tie nodded at them. "Welcome to Club Inferno."

Kat didn't look around in curiosity, her gaze on the male in front of them. Still, she telepathically said, *This...isn't what I expected.*

The entryway was designed to look like the most boring hotel lobby ever created. Two mirror image sitting areas were to the right and left of them. Both had cubed couches positioned around an oversized ottoman. A chandelier hung above each section, and sleep-inducing classical music streamed through from hidden speakers. Even the scent was sterile, clinical. *It's a façade. Just wait. You'll get to see all sorts of kink, I promise.* He swore she was feline sometimes for how curious she was about everything.

He felt her laughter along their telepathic link.

"I'm here to see Ferguson," he said, setting the bundle of weapons on the floor next to him. No reason to play games. And he knew the owner of this club was watching from multiple hidden cameras, could hear everything being said right now.

The guard's gaze scanned Kat and even though Ferguson's people were usually professional the male's eyes widened ever so slightly as he got a full look at her. His vampire eyes went bright amber as he nodded at them, his gaze lingering on her.

Jayce's wolf was secure that Kat was his, but he didn't like the way this male looked at his mate. Keeping a neutral expression, he somehow resisted flashing his canines.

"No weapons allowed past this point," the male said, looking between the two of them.

"You can keep the ones on the floor, but my blades come with me." Certain rules didn't apply to him. And if Ferguson thought he'd try to enforce that bullshit on Jayce, he'd see how dirty Jayce could play.

He paused, as if listening to instructions, then nodded. "Fine, but I need to search her." A hint of lust glinted in his gaze.

Before Jayce could respond, Kat's canines descended. Her expression was cold, her pale blue eyes shards of ice. "Touch me and you'll lose an important part of your anatomy."

Jayce's wolf grinned in approval. Hell yeah, that was his mate.

The male paused again, a new wariness setting in as he eyed them. *Yeah, that's right, fucker.* His mate was more than just pretty arm candy. She could take care of herself. Which was sexy as hell.

Before he could respond, Jayce said, "Ferguson, we need to talk. If you make me wait, I'm going to burn this place to the ground." It wasn't likely he'd take such extreme measures but he'd built a reputation as a lethal predator. And Ferguson had been ignoring his attempts at contacting him.

Jayce would not tolerate that.

After a few long moments, the male nodded then gestured to the right at what looked like a framed-out panel, but Jayce knew was actually a door. "Through there."

Dismissing the guard entirely, he and Kat headed through the door after one quick push. Once in the hallway he could feel the beat of music coming from the club. The place was broken up into sections. The softer activities were at the front, progressing onto harder things, mostly in enclosed and monitored areas.

Ferguson might be an asshole but he took care of his patrons.

The art is incredible, Kat murmured along their link.

This particular hallway had oil paintings framed in gold, all erotic in nature. Mostly nude females and males alone in sensual poses with a few ménage images. Tame for what went on behind closed doors.

This is his private hallway to his private office.

The hallway ended at an enforced door that opened as they reached it. After descending two flights of stairs, they stopped at another door, went through a bland waiting area straight to the open door of Ferguson's personal office.

It looked the same as it had before, like a CEO's boardroom.

I'm feeling insanely disappointed right now. Kat's voice was a grumble in his head. *This is a sex club. I thought he'd have naked men and women... doing stuff.*

Jayce fought a grin. Before Kat he'd had little humor in his life. Never had to fight to keep his control. Around her, however, he felt alive in a way he never had before, and she amused him at the most inopportune times. She was his north star.

He cleared his throat as Ferguson rose from the chair behind his desk. Wearing a custom-made suit, the pale-skinned man—pale even by vampire standards—gave him a sharp look, his green eyes cold. "To what do I owe this pleasure?" There was no inflection in his voice as he rounded the desk, leaned against the front of it.

Jayce wouldn't bother with niceties. The other male wouldn't appreciate them. That was the good thing about the supernatural races. You could cut through all the bullshit. "Arthur Adamson is missing. His last known location was this club. I want the video feeds the night he went missing until now."

Ferguson's jaw tightened. "My patrons value their privacy."

"I'm working on The Council's behalf as well as the Brethren's. Give me the feeds or we'll have an issue." He didn't have the time or the inclination to feign civility with this male. "Do you really want to push me?" The question came out more animal than man. His wolf flared in his gaze as he watched the other male.

Though he kept his stance neutral, he was poised for an attack, ready to strike out hard and fast if this fool thought he could come at him.

Chapter 14

Aldric kept his hand on the small of Natalia's back as they made their way through the club. It didn't matter that clothing separated them—he felt the heat of her, wanted to stroke her everywhere. Niko also had his hand on her back, but Aldric ignored that. They were caging her in and the diamond collar she wore was a clear sign she belonged to them.

He didn't want to collar her, didn't want to cage her, he just wanted her for always. But in a place like this it needed to be clear she belonged to someone so others would stay away. He didn't have the patience to be civil to any assholes who might want to approach her. Right now he was on a wire's edge of control.

After dealing with the vampire at the front, they'd been permitted into the interior of the club and were now making their way to the private room they'd reserved.

The same room Arthur had reserved the night he went missing.

Natalia didn't pause as they passed a roped-off area where a bound woman was being pleasured by multiple partners while completely immobile, but he could feel the tension humming through her. He knew she didn't have much experience, wondered what she thought of everything.

He'd been to places like this when on the job, and Niko had too, but this would be a shock to her senses. He couldn't help but wonder if she liked it. His wolf hated the idea of any exhibition where she was concerned. Most possessive, dominant shifters did. They didn't share.

If Natalia were his, he would *never* share her. Ever. He'd shred anyone who thought to take her away from him. The scent of sex was thick in the air, was agitating his wolf, pushing that need to claim Natalia even harder.

Vamps were a very different species. While he'd sensed a few shifters here tonight, the majority in this place were vampires.

"Why do some of the vamps have different patches?" she murmured, looking up at Niko.

Aldric wished she'd turned to him.

"They signify which club they belong to. The red and black ones mean they're members here but anything else means they're members of another one."

They passed a wall of circular windows that gave a glimpse into rooms where people were being whipped or caned. Natalia's eyes widened slightly as they passed but there were too many scents in this place for him to guess what she was thinking other than pure shock.

The female who led them to a hallway of private rooms turned and gave Natalia a flirty smile as they reached the room. "If you're ever looking for a female partner, let me know."

Even as Aldric's possessiveness shoved to the surface, Natalia's cheeks tinged the sexiest shade of pink as she nodded. He didn't care if it was male or female hitting on her, he didn't like it. Especially now when she was barely clothed and looked good enough to eat. The red dress she had on was simple and sexy. It had some sort of lace overlay, hugged all her curves and might as well have been created for her and her alone.

Once they were inside, Aldric locked the door behind them, but no one said anything. He was fairly certain the rooms weren't under video surveillance—because if they were and anyone found out, Ferguson would be dead. But that didn't mean they wouldn't do their due diligence.

They needed to search the room regardless. This was the last place Arthur had been seen and though it was a long shot, they were still looking for clues.

That was the thing about his job: investigative work was long and tedious most of the time.

Right now he was struggling to keep his mind on the task at hand, something he'd never suffered from before. His work had always kept him focused, with a purpose. With Natalia here tonight, in the last type of place he'd ever take her, too many emotions warred inside him.

His wolf was oddly content having Natalia nearby, always had been. He'd desperately missed her the last five and a half months. Had wondered what she'd been doing—and who with. When he'd been away from her, it had been as if he'd been missing an integral part of himself.

He knew why, but had wanted to deny it. Because he felt... guilty. As if he was betraying a ghost long gone from this plane of existence. A female he hadn't thought about since he'd met Natalia. That was what shredded him inside. He had no right to be happy, not after his failures as a mate. He'd been carrying around the weight of his failure for so fucking long.

Until Natalia. Then he'd allowed himself to feel something more, to let her in. To wonder if maybe they could have something more than friendship. Of course he'd fucked all of it up.

Shaking that thought off, he went to the California-king-sized bed and bent to check under it. It was an obvious place to hide something, but he wouldn't overlook it because of laziness.

The three of them worked silently, covering every inch of the lush room. The erotic art on the walls was incredibly obscene sketches done in charcoal. The bedding was all blacks, reds and...hideous. He didn't like her being in a place like this, but now that they were in work mode she didn't even seem to care that they were in a sex club. All traces of her shock from earlier were gone.

As Natalia moved to one side of a huge gold-framed mirror, he moved to the other. They slightly lifted it away from the wall and were able to see that it was a regular mirror, not a two-way.

Natalia completely ignored him, refusing to make eye contact with him and it was all he could do to keep his gaze off her. He wished it was just the two of them right now, that Niko wasn't part of this investigation.

God, he'd fucked up but good. He might have made the decision to court her, but that didn't mean anything right now. He had a long road in front of him. He'd broken their friendship and now he had to build it up again.

He wanted far more than friendship, but that would be a later step. Getting her to simply forgive him would be the first hurdle. The guilt still raged inside him, that he was doing something wrong and betraying the memory of his dead mate, but the sheer need to keep Natalia, to possess her, overrode it.

When she moved to another wall, standing on tiptoe to run her fingers under one of the framed sketches, he froze, watching the way her short dress lifted, skimming the curve of her ass. He rolled his shoulders once, all the muscles in his body pulling taut.

He'd seen her naked in the past after a shift to human form and it only made him fantasize more about stripping her down, claiming her.

Because she already owned him. Even if he'd been too stupid to realize it until last night.

When he sensed Niko watching him, he flashed his canines at the male. It didn't matter that he knew nothing had happened between him and Natalia—his wolf was being a dick.

Niko responded with a flash of fangs before returning to searching through a drawer of sex toys in new packaging.

When Natalia bent over to inspect something at the base of the bed, he groaned at the flash of her smooth, bronze ass. Either she was wearing nothing or a thong, and clearly trying to make him crazy. Not intentionally though because he knew she wasn't like that.

Before either of them could turn toward him and see why he'd groaned, he swiveled to the nearest piece of furniture and began inspecting it.

"Oh!"

He turned at the sound of Natalia's excitement—to see a hidden door open right next to the bed.

"I pressed that by accident," she said to the two of them, pointing down at the gold inlay above the baseboard. "I was just feeling around for..." She trailed off, likely in case there were any sort of audio recorders in place. If there was visual it wouldn't matter at this point.

He bent down to inspect the small section of the gold inlay she'd depressed. "This is good craftsmanship." The seam was almost invisible.

"He could have left from here," Niko said.

"Or been forcibly taken." Aldric's voice was grim as he stood to face the male.

Niko simply nodded, his expression mirroring Aldric's.

Natalia placed her hands on her hips. "Well, let's go, then. See where this leads."

"You want to take the lead?" he asked Niko. Because no way would she be leading or taking up the back.

His wolf might be agitated by Niko right now, but this male would help protect her.

Niko lifted a shoulder. "I'll go first."

That was interesting. And a show of trust that Aldric didn't deserve. Niko would be putting his back to him. After the way he'd attacked the male, Niko had every right to demand to be behind Aldric. This could be his way of telling Aldric he didn't view him as a threat—an insult—but Aldric didn't think so.

Fuck. He needed to apologize to the male. Later, he swore. Aldric nodded and Niko headed into a tunnel, followed by Natalia, then him. Senses on alert, he scanned their surroundings even as he inhaled, searching for anything that might be a threat.

She moved like a soldier, just as alert as they were. Natalia might be petite and delicate-looking but the female was a fighter.

The glow of Niko's gaze lit up the tunnel in front of him, but neither Aldric nor Natalia needed it. Not with their own night vision.

The concrete of the tunnel and floor was smooth, clearly man-made. As they silently strode through it he heard the soft whoosh of the door closing behind them.

So there was about a twenty second window before it closed.

Inhaling, he sifted through the scents surrounding them, dismissing Natalia and Niko's scents. The smell of the club's owner was down here, as if he used this tunnel often. It was more of a lingering aroma, embedded into the stone.

A few other odors drifted on the air, including Arthur's, but not recent. If he'd been here a week ago, that was about right. At least now Aldric knew how the male had left the club.

Whether he'd been forced or not remained to be discovered.

From the fairly straight direction they were headed he didn't think they were moving deeper underground but he pulled out his cell phone as they continued on, saw that he still had service.

In front of him, Natalia marched on silently. She'd worn heels with added rubber soles in case they had to be stealthy. She might be young, but she was still a predator and she'd learned how to sneak up on prey long before she'd met him. It was one of the reasons he'd liked bringing her with him on hunts. One of the least important reasons.

Even if she hadn't been able to handle herself, that was something he could have taught her. He just liked being around her. She had enough passion and fire inside her for an entire pack. The female was...incredible.

Right now her scent was making his wolf want to rub up against her. Her mere presence had this way of making him forget about everything else.

When the temperature changed slightly, the three of them slowed, a cohesive unit. Niko held up a hand, motioning that the exit was coming up, but Aldric could see the faint outline anyway.

Niko moved carefully out of the tunnel and even though Aldric knew it would make Natalia crazy, he edged in front of her. She wouldn't make a stink about it because she wouldn't want to draw attention to them if anyone was waiting to ambush them.

The likelihood of that seemed slim but he didn't care. Protecting her was all that mattered and he'd do it with his life.

Tension rolled off her, but as he predicted, she didn't try to shove in front of him, instead letting him move out with Niko into...an empty warehouse.

Chapter 15

Ferguson opened his palm and handed Jayce a flash drive. "All the files you require. We don't have feeds in any of the rooms, but there are recordings in the main areas for the time you want. Now get the fuck out of my club." He didn't move from his position against the desk as he stared at Jayce, his expression dark.

Jayce took the flash drive, not surprised the male had it ready for him despite his bullshit about patrons valuing their privacy. "Who was Arthur meeting with the night he was here?"

"None of your fucking business."

Jayce's canines descended. Some beings only respected raw strength. He hadn't wanted to resort to violence tonight, but Ferguson was apparently in the mood to make things difficult. Before Jayce could think about making a move, Kat said, "Tell my mate what he wants to know, or I'll make your life difficult."

Damn it, Kat. He knew where she was going with this, had told her that would be a last resort. Because Jayce could handle this fucker. Sure, it would get bloody, but that was just part of the job.

As she spoke, she sat on one of the velour tufted chairs in front of the desk. She crossed her long, lean legs and gave him a haughty look.

Ferguson looked at Kat for the first time with what could be considered amusement. "I'd heard you'd gotten mated. Tell me, *child*, how will you make my life difficult?" That same amusement in his gaze was mirrored in his voice as he looked at Kat, not with lust—as most males tended to do—but disdain. He was definitely stronger than Kat, though probably not as strong as he thought.

Her scent was that of a young wolf, but he'd been training with her. People would always underestimate her because of her age and that was a good thing.

But Kat wasn't going to attack Ferguson physically—not that Jayce would let that happen regardless. She was going for the metaphorical jugular. Jayce gritted his teeth, knowing he couldn't stop her now that she'd started.

"I'll disrupt some of your weapons supply lines. Most of them, actually." The haughty look was gone, replaced by an icy, pure lupine stare. "Even if you give Jayce what he wants, I still might do it for the child comment."

Ferguson laughed with raw amusement as he looked at Jayce. "Your mate's a fucking comedian."

Kat's voice sliced through the room like a whip. "Before I became Katarina Kazan, I was Katarina Saburova. And my father will be very angry at the disrespect you've shown us tonight." Even before she'd become a shifter, Kat had always understood that you had to show fearlessness in the face of some people, that they only understood strength. She wasn't lying either. She'd do exactly what she said. And Ferguson would smell the truth on her.

All amusement fled Ferguson's pale face. It took him two seconds to figure out who she was. Kat's father was one of the most brutal arms dealers on the planet. He was *not* a good man, but he'd protected his daughter. So much so that most people didn't even realize he had one. It didn't matter that he was human—supernaturals feared him because of the power he wielded. And Ferguson used Saburova for some of his weapons dealing. The vampire wasn't just a sex club owner. No, he had his fingers in many pots—many illegal ones.

Ferguson cleared his throat and spoke to Jayce. "He wasn't meeting anyone here. He wanted use of one of my rooms because..." He gritted his teeth as he visibly had to shove back his anger. "There's a hidden exit. He wanted to make sure he wasn't followed to a meeting. I have no idea where he was going after he left. I swear on my honor."

Jayce didn't scent a lie, and Ferguson swearing on his honor was a big deal for vampires and shifters alike.

"Is there anything else relevant about Arthur we need to know? Anything at all? I don't want to come back here." Jayce's voice was low. Because if this male held something back, the next time Jayce returned, he'd make good on his promise to burn the place down. As the enforcer for his region, he could never appear weak, always had to back up his words with action. He didn't utter threats. He delivered promises.

"No, but I will show you to the room so you can see the exit. I believe it's currently occupied but I can have my staff relocate whoever is in there." His voice was butter-smooth politeness now as he looked at both Jayce and Kat.

His acquiescence was slightly nauseating. Jayce's wolf had been all geared up for a fight.

He kept his expression neutral. It was occupied, all right. He wouldn't reveal to Arthur that he knew the occupants of the room. If he needed someone to infiltrate the club again, Niko, Natalia and Aldric could return undetected.

Kat stood, even as Jayce moved to put his body between hers and Ferguson's. He didn't think the vampire was foolish enough to try to attack her, but Jayce's wolf was agitated right now. He didn't like that she'd given away who she was.

His aura is all muddy. A mix of reds and brown.

Jayce gritted his teeth, didn't respond along their telepathic link. Kat saw auras when she looked at people. It was part of her seer gift. Red was often anger and brown could represent fear. The two colors made sense.

"Lead the way," he ordered the male.

Why did you do that? Anger growled in his telepathic link to Kat as they followed the vampire.

Kat linked her hand through his arm, her grip possessive. *Because I know you don't like hurting people in front of me. And that guy was about to get his face bashed in. It doesn't bother me, even if you think it does. But I hurt when you're in distress. If I can save you even a minute's worth of pain, I'll do it. I'm your mate. I get to take care of you. So don't argue with me.*

His throat tightened so much he couldn't even respond telepathically for a moment. Until her, he hadn't known this kind of love was possible. It had changed him. *You make it hard to be angry at you.*

He felt her pleasure along their link, like the sweetest, softest caress against his senses. He couldn't wait to get her back to the B&B, to show her exactly what she meant to him.

Chapter 16

Natalia tried not to fidget as they waited for Kat and Jayce in the SUV. Aldric had texted Jayce to tell him they'd found a secret exit, and it turned out he and Kat were heading out that same way.

After exiting through the tunnel, they'd found nothing in that warehouse. Not even a lone homeless person. If Natalia had to guess, it was because the owner of the sex club monitored it, at least occasionally. They hadn't discovered any security cameras in the building but that didn't mean they weren't there.

"I see them," Aldric murmured from the driver's seat, starting the SUV's engine. She was sitting in the front with him only to let Kat and Jayce sit together—and because Niko hadn't wanted to sit in front with Aldric.

Moments later the two of them slid into the backseat after Aldric stopped beside them on the sidewalk. He was moving again before they'd settled in.

"What did that dick say?" Aldric asked, steering smoothly down the street.

Natalia tried not to notice the flex of his arm muscles or his intoxicating scent. If she let her emotions get away from her, she'd get all turned on by him and everyone in the vehicle would know it. That was beyond embarrassing. She'd already had to keep herself in check in the club. All those sights and scents had been overwhelming. She wasn't used to being around that many new people or in such an enclosed space. She'd seen her share of naked bodies, considering she was a shifter, but...she'd never witnessed people doing so many different *things* to each other. Seeing all that had been erotic. Combined with the feel of Aldric's hand on her back, she'd been ready to turn into his arms and rub up against him.

Her wolf wasn't happy with her right now.

But she was still keeping an emotional distance from him. Even if she could be professional for this job, it didn't mean she had to let him back into her life.

"He gave me the video footage we need, but aside from that, he doesn't know anything other than Arthur wanted to use his club as a way to leave undetected on the way to a meeting. Ferguson didn't seem to think Arthur was particularly worried he was being followed. He was just being cautious. Dickhead doesn't know who he was meeting with, either."

"I got some names from Ursula. Potential enemies of both Arthur and Darius. Combined with the list of people we already have who're most likely to want an alliance between the Kinley pack and Clifton coven to fail, there are overlapping names. I've also got some new names from Ursula, vampires who know about Constance and Darius. Names that weren't on Constance's list."

"You think Constance left names off intentionally?" Natalia asked. She hadn't met the shifter female and had no way to gauge if she was trustworthy.

Aldric shook his head. "I don't think the shifter princess left the names off her own list. I don't think she realizes these vamps know of her relationship."

"You want to start with the vampires who are privy to their relationship?" Jayce asked.

Aldric nodded. "Combined with what I've already got, the list isn't long. I can knock out most of it tonight."

"Natalia, you want to go with Aldric? You two work well together and you put people at ease," Jayce said.

Natalia's instinct was to say hell no, but she nodded. This job was important to her. She was an adult and could work with Aldric, at least right now. Finding out who had taken the two vampires, and stopping a powerful coven and pack from going to war was important to all their people. She wouldn't let her personal feelings get in the way of that. "Of course."

Jayce nodded and turned to Niko and Kat, talking about the way they would divide up the other names. She tuned them out even as she tried to squash the annoying thrill of her wolf that she'd get to spend time alone with Aldric.

Traitorous bitch, she grumbled to herself. *We are not happy with him right now.* From the time she was a pup, her wolf and human side had always been as one, in agreement on everything.

Until now.

Her wolf wanted to jump Aldric, to completely lose control with the male, with skin-on-skin contact. And Natalia mainly wanted to punch him in the face.

***

"Niko is so different than the last few vampires we talked to. All the vampires I've met, actually—except Larissa. Do you know why?" she asked Aldric a couple hours later. She didn't know much about vampires. Even in college she hadn't met any.

It was just her and Aldric now, and though she was angry at him, she wasn't going to drive around in silence. They'd already visited three of the twelve vampires on his list so far. They were making good progress. It helped that the coven members lived in the same exclusive neighborhood.

"That's a complex answer. One on one, vamps are just as different as shifters or humans. If a vamp was an asshole when they were turned, they're simply an asshole vampire instead of an asshole human. This isn't scientific, but many vampires view humans as food. I think it skews the way they look at the world, compared to the way shifters do. Humans aren't prey to us."

"I never thought about it like that."

He shrugged. "Another theory is that vamps tend to attract like-minded people to them."

"So assholes are going to create assholes? Is that what you mean?" Most vampires were turned, though the most powerful were bloodborn. For vampires to procreate was incredibly rare and those who were born vampires were powerful beyond measure.

"More or less."

"Larissa's not like that though."

"I've met many vampires and I can say that she and Niko are anomalies. Her especially, given her power level."

Natalia liked the powerful vampire who'd mated with one of her packmates. Though she could admit the female's powers were a little terrifying. As the daughter of Vlad the Impaler, it was to be expected though. "Did you know the Brethren asked her to join them again?" They'd asked once before almost six months ago and Larissa had said no.

Aldric rolled his eyes. "No, but I'm not surprised. They'll keep asking until they think she really means no."

"You don't think she does?"

"I think she'd be a good addition to the group. And it would create a link between The Council and the Brethren since she's mated to a shifter. A connection like that will only be good for our kind. And for your pack."

"That's not exactly an answer, but yeah, I don't see a downside to her joining them. I think she might actually consider it in a few years. But she's just been reunited with her mate. I don't blame her for not wanting to take on a bunch of political bullshit." The woman had been in a virtual coma for decades, separated from her mate. She had a right to live her life.

"This is the next place on the list," Aldric said, pulling into a driveway of another huge home. He put the vehicle in park.

She wasn't sure why vampires needed so much damn space when they didn't tend to mate and have young like shifters did. "Their homes are ridiculous."

He snorted. "It's a vampire thing. I don't get it either."

Being with him like this, and talking like they used to, was a slap of icy water in her face. She didn't want to fall into the trap of relaxing with him, of letting him in any more than she already had. She would be professional, but that didn't mean she could let her guard down with him. She had to remember that.

"Oh, I got something for you." He opened the center console to reveal a bag of cheddar popcorn. One of her favorites.

"Thank you." The words came out stilted, awkward. Maybe she couldn't do this, couldn't work with him. Yeah, she was an adult, but she wasn't a robot. The Aldric who'd been her friend had always plied her with her favorite snacks on their stakeouts, had teased her about her love of Lifetime movies. "Aldric, I..." Trailing off, she wasn't sure how to continue. She didn't want to argue with him, but she was still hurting deep inside.

"I'm so fucking sorry for everything, Natalia." His words were raspy and when she met his gray-green eyes she could see raw pain there.

It wasn't the time or place but... "What exactly are you sorry for?" she demanded, the thin grasp on her emotions shredding.

"I'm sorry for cutting you out of my life." His voice was ragged, his expression miserable. "That last morning at your house, I..." He cleared his throat. "I'm sorry for hurting you."

Truth was in every word, but she needed real answers. "Why did you do it?" Tears stung her eyes and even though she hated the show of weakness, she couldn't pretend to be unaffected. He'd shredded her apart. She'd recently lost her parents, cousins and other packmates to a mass murderer. Then her own sister had almost been killed by a psychopathic vampire. Aldric's leaving had been like pouring acid on her already bruised heart. On a completely different level. Deeper, because it had been from Aldric, because he'd made the damn *choice* to leave her.

"I got scared."

She laughed at the ludicrousness of his words. She couldn't imagine him afraid of anything. "Of what?"

"You." He scrubbed a hand over the back of his neck but held her gaze. "I wanted to take you right up against the front door," he growled out.

His words ignited a firestorm inside her. He said it like it was a bad thing. But the thought of him losing control, taking her the way her body craved... *Nope.* She ruthlessly shoved back all those thoughts. Even letting her mind travel down that path meant she was going to get way too turned on. And he'd scent it. Her throat was too tight to respond but luckily he continued.

"I acted like a fucking coward. I've been roaming for centuries and you're one of the first people I let into my life. You're one of the sweetest females I've ever known. I... I don't deserve your friendship, but I'm asking for a second chance. And I'm asking for your forgiveness."

Friendship? Her tears dried at that word. Swallowing hard, she didn't respond right away as she tried to get her thoughts together. When it came down to it, she had a feeling he'd never get over his dead mate. He hadn't come out and said it, but all he was asking for right now was friendship—after he'd *admitted* his sexual attraction to her. He'd never be free of his past and she simply couldn't wait and hope for anything more. It wasn't like he ever talked about his dead mate either. So she had no idea what was going on in his head.

Pining after someone who could never give her what she needed was too painful, and fuck that—she deserved to come first in her mate's life. Now it was glaringly clear that Aldric didn't *want* to want her sexually, he just wanted what they'd had before. Simple, platonic friendship. The knowledge made her stomach tighten. And the truth was, she didn't freaking trust him anymore. What if he panicked again and decided she wasn't important to him anymore? *Nope.*

"I do forgive you." Because he was sincere and she simply couldn't hold a grudge. Not when it was clear he was hurting. "But I don't know if we can ever go back to what we had. It comes down to trust, you know? After this job, I think maybe... I think I don't want to work with you again. And I can't be friends with you." The words came out raspy, but they needed to be said.

It hurt too much.

He nodded, his jaw tight. His eyes went wolf, making it impossible for her to read him.

Multiple lights in front of the house flicked on, drawing their attention to it. Yeah, sitting out in a vampire's driveway and having this conversation was probably not the best timing.

"You ready?" she asked, opening her door. She was desperate to escape the confining vehicle, and the way his scent wrapped around her made her crazy.

Wordlessly he followed suit and they headed up the stone walkway to the ornate front door.

Locking all of her emotions up tight, Natalia mentally prepared for another vampire meeting. It was time to work, not feel sorry for herself.

Chapter 17

Aldric didn't want to be here, didn't want to deal with questioning any more vampires tonight. They had hours and hours of investigation left. At least he was with Natalia, though it was heaven and torture.

The truth in her eyes when she told him she didn't want to work with him after this job, didn't even want to be his friend, was a slice directly to his heart. He wasn't giving up on claiming her, but the reality of what he'd done to their relationship settled into his bones, weighing him down.

As they reached the front door, it opened. Leigh Dawson, a fairly young vampire of one hundred, nodded once at Aldric and stepped back. "Welcome to our home," he said, looking at Natalia. "I'm Leigh, but you already know that."

"Natalia," she said, nodding politely.

The most feral part of Aldric was glad they didn't shake hands. It was caveman but he didn't want her touching any other males. After the sex club they'd been to earlier, he wanted to wash the stink of it off both of them. "Thank you for agreeing to see us on such short notice."

Leigh snorted. "Don't have a choice, do we?"

Aldric lifted a shoulder. "You always have a choice." Of course if he'd rejected Aldric's request it would have put him on the Brethren's radar, something no vampire wanted.

The male's jaw tightened as he led them down a long hallway and into a plush study. His mate, Ivonne, was already waiting, wearing gray slacks, a silky white top and a gray cardigan. Her pale blonde hair was down around her delicate face. Leigh stood next to her, his light brown skin a contrast to her ivory coloring.

"Aldric. Welcome to our home." Her voice was crisp. "Can we offer either of you refreshments?"

Aldric shook his head and quickly introduced Natalia before asking if they could all sit. Standing didn't bother him, but it seemed to make people uneasy. Right now he wanted the vampires as relaxed as possible. It wasn't as if he thought they'd spill all their secrets because they were sitting, but putting people at ease would only help this investigation.

Leigh went to get drinks for him and his mate as the three of them sat around a huge leather ottoman. Across from Aldric and Natalia, Ivonne gave him a once-over, her hunger crystal clear as she swept her gaze over his chest and lower.

Next to him Natalia stiffened ever so slightly. It didn't go unnoticed by the female vampire, who paused before leaning back in her chair.

Aldric would never understand that facet of the vampire species. Not all of them had open relationships, but he'd met enough vamps that he knew it was common enough for mates to stray or bring others into the relationship.

"If it's all right with the two of you," Aldric said as Leigh sat next to his mate, handing her a glass of blood, "I'd like to cut right to why we're here."

Both of them nodded.

"You know about the relationship between Darius and Constance."

Darkness flickered in Leigh's brown eyes. "We're aware."

"You don't like their relationship?"

Ivonne smiled and patted Leigh's thigh. "It's not that he doesn't approve of interspecies matings, it's just..."

"The two of them think that their mating will bond our coven and their pack?" Leigh gave a derisive snort.

"And you don't?"

"There's too much bad blood between our people."

"So you want a war, then?" Aldric asked.

"I didn't say that. We're just as tired of fighting as they are. But I don't like this bullshit mating idea." All his muscles were pulled taut, his mate patting his leg gently.

From what Aldric understood, the mating wasn't bullshit, wasn't contrived.

Or it would be real if they finished bonding. First they had to *find* Darius. Aldric wasn't going to bother arguing with this male though. That wasn't why he was here. He simply needed to gather information. Anything that might help him locate the two missing males. "How did you first find out about the potential mating? It's not common knowledge."

Ivonne shrugged. "Arthur came to us about it. Our opinion has sway with the coven and he wanted to see how receptive we'd be to the idea of one of our own mating with a Kinley."

"It was clear his question wasn't hypothetical, so I pushed." Leigh lifted a shoulder. "He eventually told us."

"Arthur is supportive of the joining," Aldric continued. "Did that make you angry?"

Leigh's brow furrowed. "Why would it make me angry?"

"That's not an answer." Vampires were just as evasive as shifters when they didn't want to directly answer a question.

Leigh shoved up from his seat. "Why the fuck are you asking me all these questions?"

Ivonne tugged on his wrist gently, her expression growing strained. There was such an age difference between these two. From the files he had on the two of them, Ivonne was centuries older. She seemed to be able to control his moods at least.

Aldric leaned back in his chair, keeping his cool when it was clear this male had control issues. Before he could ask his next question, Natalia spoke.

"How many of your staff are here right now, able to listen in on this conversation?" Her voice was calm, but Aldric sensed her anger under the surface. She was incredible at scenting out things, another reason she was so good on investigations.

Subtly, he inhaled but didn't scent anyone else—yet there were many smells to sift through in here, including various cleaners. He'd specifically told Ivonne and Leigh before arriving that they should be the only two in residence. However...he realized there was a very faint heartbeat coming from somewhere.

Aldric and Natalia stood almost in unison and whatever was on their faces made Leigh return to his seat.

Ivonne sighed, seemingly unconcerned. "Crystal, please come in here." Her voice was raised only slightly.

A woman wearing what was clearly a cleaning uniform strode in a few moments later, her eyes wide as she looked at Aldric. When she made eye contact with him her fangs descended once before she pulled them back in. A natural instinct for some when faced with a predator.

"You're Crystal?" he asked.

The woman was tall like Ivonne, the scent of her faint. Even with her in the same room he could barely smell her. He wondered how Natalia had picked up on her presence even as he cursed himself for having not.

"Yes. I clean here three times a week." She shot a wary gaze to Ivonne then looked back at Aldric.

"Could you hear our conversation?"

Swallowing, she nodded. "Yes."

Well, hell. "Return to whatever you were doing but don't leave just yet. I need to talk to you." Angry at the disrespect shown to him on multiple levels, Aldric turned back to the couple. His wolf was in his gaze and his voice. "I'm going to need a list of every single person in your home, whether staff or visitors, over the last six months."

Leigh's expression turned murderous but Ivonne squeezed his leg before standing. "I'll make you a list."

Aldric could understand general annoyance at being questioned in your own home and being unable to ask specific questions of the investigator, but Leigh's behavior had just put him at the top of Aldric's shit list. Not only had he lied to them, but now their suspect list had grown even bigger. Most vampires tended to keep their business private but apparently these two morons thought it was okay to talk about confidential things with staff around. Stupid.

Thirty minutes later, after questioning the vampire couple, the cleaning woman and obtaining a list from Ivonne, Aldric and Natalia headed out. They still had more stops to make before sunrise.

"Why did you think there was someone else in the house?" he asked as he steered out of the driveway. He hated that he hadn't scented Crystal.

"The scent of fresh lemon cleaner. It was down the hallway and in the study. It was too fresh so I knew someone had been cleaning very recently. And you know that bitch doesn't clean her own house."

He laughed. "Bitch?"

Natalia shot him a sideways glance. "I didn't like her. She was checking you out with her mate in the same room. That's disrespectful."

Aldric's primal side was smug with satisfaction at the hint of possessiveness in Natalia's voice. He didn't know if she was even aware of it but he heard it, *felt* it, straight to his core.

It told him that maybe things weren't quite as impossible between them as he'd feared. He wasn't giving up, regardless.

Not where Natalia was concerned.

He would win her trust first. This female was his, and once he claimed her there was no going back.

Chapter 18

Moving quickly and quietly she hurried through the woods. It would be dawn soon and she needed to check on her captives. She wasn't worried about them escaping but both Arthur and Darius were powerful males. So she couldn't underestimate them.

Too bad they'd been stupid enough to underestimate her. Like most males, regardless of the species. Now they were going to help her bring the Kinley Alpha down. She wasn't foolish enough to think she could dismantle the entire Kinley pack, but she *could* hurt the Alpha. He deserved every ounce of pain she could give him.

The best way to hurt that animal was to kill his daughter.

And she had the best plan laid out to have that haughty bitch executed. Years in the making, her plan was finally coming together. But she had to be smart, take things one step at a time.

With her mask and other clothing in place, she was hidden from head to toe. She couldn't hide that she was a female but that didn't matter. After scanning the forest, she moved the underbrush off the trapdoor and opened it.

The twilight sky offered enough illumination, but she didn't need it. Not with her extrasensory abilities. After opening the door she waited, listened.

She could hear faint shuffling coming from the prison she'd created. The prison no one knew about. It had taken decades to get it built, to get everything right.

She was near immortal so she'd had the time. If anything, the more centuries that passed, the more her need for vengeance had grown. She would never let go of her anger, her rage.

So she'd turned that rage into an ice-cold blade and she wouldn't be satisfied until the male who had killed her mate was utterly destroyed. Because outliving the only male she'd ever loved was worse than death. Something that monster Craig Kinley would soon learn. Losing his daughter would destroy him.

If she played things right, no one would ever know what she'd done. And the Alpha would have to live with the fact that his daughter was dead and there was nothing he could do to bring her back—and that he'd been helpless to save her.

It had to happen according to her plan. Not a simple kill. No, Constance would be framed and executed for her 'crimes.' Only later would it be revealed that the little bitch hadn't been guilty at all.

That would shred the Kinley Alpha. His daughter would be dead, and all for nothing.

It would probably start a war, but she didn't give a shit. She'd been alive a long time. She wasn't afraid of death and she was willing to die if it brought her deceased mate justice.

Not bothering with the ladder, she pulled the door shut over her, then jumped down the ten feet to the solid concrete ground. The prison was perfect and insulated. And it was far enough away from prying ears that no one would hear shouts of help.

Both males were sitting up, each on the mattress she'd left inside their individual cells. She wasn't a complete monster.

They watched her carefully, wordlessly as she stood in front of the bars to their prison. Quickly scanning, she didn't see any damage anywhere. Well, not much. Some of the concrete near both prison doors was crumbled away, as if the males had tried to pound their way under the doors using their fists.

She'd thought of that though and didn't comment on their pathetic escape attempts. No need to. They wouldn't be escaping.

She tossed a blood bag first into Darius's cell, then into Arthur's. When neither made a move to go for their bags, she took a step closer—but not so close that she was within reach of the bars. "Drink it," she whispered. "If I'd wanted you dead, you would be already." When they still didn't move, she continued. "If you don't, I'll bring a live human down here, cut her open and you can fight your hunger to drink from her until it's too much. Which will be worse? Being drugged, or killing a defenseless little human?" She kept her words almost subvocal, so quiet they wouldn't be able to make out her identity.

Her words had the impact she was looking for because both males picked up their blood bags, hate clear in their gazes.

"Drink," she hissed. Her gold mask covered any facial expressions that might give her away as well.

Growling, both males picked up their bags and with a quick puncture from their fangs, they started sucking them dry.

Satisfied that they'd be unconscious soon, she turned and headed back the way she'd come. She couldn't be gone long right now. It was almost dawn and as it was she'd been cutting it close getting here. But she'd wanted to make sure they were unconscious or at least weakened for the next twelve hours. She'd increased the dosage of the drugs this time.

Just because she'd fortified this place didn't mean it was escape-proof. She was almost certain it was, but she might have missed something. And she hadn't had a chance to test it before now so she was covering all her bases.

Hurrying back up the ladder, she paused as she slowly pushed the trapdoor up. Inhaling deeply, she took in all the scents of the forest. No vampires or shifters nearby. No humans either, but that was a given. No humans were stupid enough to venture into this territory.

Using her supernatural speed, she jumped out and secured the trapdoor before racing back home. Orange streaks were already painting the sky, urging her to go faster, faster. Normally she'd prefer to lay a scent trail somewhere else then return home by other means, but there was no time.

She hadn't been able to visit the males earlier because of the stupid shifters skulking everywhere. She knew they'd been hired by both the Brethren and The Council, though she wasn't certain if they knew Darius was missing yet.

She assumed so but there had been no official announcement anywhere. It would come soon, she was certain.

Adrenaline raced through her veins. She needed to feed, to sleep. Then when the sun set again, it was on to the next part of her plan. This next step would be a bit messier, but she didn't care. Nothing would stop her from getting her revenge.

Chapter 19

Arthur spat the blood out onto the ground as soon as the trapdoor closed. He was almost certain they were underground, not in a dungeon like he'd assumed before. An icy chill invaded the space and though the cold didn't affect him like humans, he still felt the effect on his body. Especially since he hadn't fed in a couple days.

Next to him Darius did the same then emptied his blood bag under his own mattress.

"We're underground," he said, wanting to see what Darius thought.

The other male nodded. "I smelled the forest when she opened that door."

"Any idea who she is?" Arthur kept his voice low even though he was certain she was gone. His internal clock told him dawn was approaching, so whoever she was, she'd want to find shelter. She was definitely a vampire. Her scent was masked but it had cool undertones, something he associated with his own kind.

Darius shook his head, rage vibrating off him. "We need to get out of here. I need to get to Constance."

Arthur understood the male's anguish; he was just keeping his own locked down much tighter. Darius was a younger male and hadn't yet mated. He would be more out of control with the need to get back to his female, to claim her.

Arthur refused to let fear for his mate or his own potential death make him act rashly. "Your—" He cut himself off, not wanting to say *mate* and rile the guy up more. "Constance is strong. She'll be able to take care of herself. And her father will have her guarded right now. She's safe." Something the male would know if he was thinking clearly.

Darius stood and rolled his shoulders. "I know. This entire situation is too strange. Why the fuck is that female just keeping us down here?"

Arthur knew the male wasn't looking for a real answer so he didn't respond. He moved to the door of his own cage and pounded against the concrete floor as he had during the night. Despite the level of strength he was using it barely cracked, little pieces barely crumbling off.

"She's definitely reinforced it somehow." He flexed his bruised, bloodied knuckles. They were already healing, only slightly slower than normal given that he hadn't been feeding the past week. He ignored the pain because it didn't matter.

Freedom and getting to his mate were the only things he cared about.

"My guess, she's spelled the cage as well as lined it with silver," Darius said.

Or more likely had someone—a witch, no doubt—spell it.

Arthur simply nodded, scanning his cage again. There was an invisible force stopping them from breaking through the concrete.

It was clear she'd taken their clothes to prevent them from using the material to block against the pain of silver. Pain wasn't the only thing stopping them, however, because if it would get him free he'd deal with the piercing agony. It was the risk that they'd get silver poisoning that kept him from attempting to rip the bars out.

If enough silver got into their blood it could potentially kill them, or at least disable them with enough pain that their bodies simply shut down. So they would be unconscious by the time the bitch finally returned. And without any blood to rejuvenate them if they did escape, it would be a fruitless effort.

"I'm going to try using the mattress again," Darius said.

Arthur nodded, but didn't join in with the male and try the same thing in his own cage. As he continued looking around their prison, scanning for something that might help them break free, he watched Darius out of the corner of his eye.

The male picked up his mattress and held it in front of him, using it as shield against the bars. He rammed his body against it full force.

Both their cages trembled under the impact of the blow, but there was no movement that Arthur could see.

Darius rammed into the door again and again, the shaking making it impossible for Arthur to think straight.

Breathing hard, after a few minutes the male finally stepped back. "I think it's moved a little." He shoved the mattress against the door again.

It rattled so Arthur couldn't tell one way or another. But it was better than doing nothing. He'd already tried to slam his way through the ceiling but it was coated in silver. The floor and walls were impossible to get through as well.

"Fuck," he muttered, picking up his own mattress. He could try to figure out a way to get out of here all he wanted. There simply weren't any holes in security he could see. Brute force was the only weapon they had at their disposal.

Even if he expended all his energy it didn't matter at this point. They had to get out of here. Maybe together they could break out of their cages. If they passed out, they passed out. They were already fucking helpless as it was. And he wasn't going to die in a fucking cage.

Holding the mattress in front of him just like Darius, Arthur hurled his body at the doors.

When he got free from this prison, he was going to figure out who had taken them. And make her pay.

Whoever had done this had to have an end goal. He'd been alive centuries and had seen damn near everything. Their captor had to know that taking them would draw attention from multiple sources. Everyone wanted the peace treaty to go through, including the Brethren.

Especially the Brethren.

At least people were out looking for them. Of that he had no doubt. His mate would do everything to find him.

But he couldn't depend on anyone else. Not when he had no idea what their captor's goal was. She could come back here at the next sunset and decide to burn them alive.

At that thought, he barreled at the door again, throwing all his power into breaking through the cage. Spelled or not, nothing was impenetrable.

Chapter 20

The scent of death filled Aldric's nostrils.

Faster, faster, faster. His four legs ate up the distance as he raced through the forest.

Something was wrong. His wolf scented it, felt it bone deep. Normally the familiar scent of his mate's cooking teased the air this close to their den.

Today a rusting scent seemed to permeate the air, making the most primal part of him take over.

A snarl and howl filled the air, the sound savage.

All the fur on his body stood on end but he remained quiet. That rusty iron smell grew heavier as the trees began to thin.

The den he and his mate spent time in was on the outskirts of the human village, close enough to the home they made near the humans. But they needed the forest, needed to roam in wolf form when they chose.

His small pack had declared ownership of these woods. No other shifters should be here but...something was wrong. Desperation clawed at his insides, making him move faster, faster. His father and brother weren't at their den yet because they were well behind him.

His mate was alone.

A rotting stench of the truly diseased now mixed with the scent of blood. Panic seized him, but he forced himself to think like a predator. It couldn't be his mate. It couldn't.

Moving stealthily through the trees, he kept to the shadows until he reached the clearing.

A red haze descended on his vision as blood and death greeted him. He...couldn't process what he was seeing.

His mate's severed head lay by their dwindling fire, her broken, bloody body a few feet away, her belly slashed open while a coyote ate...

No!

An anguished snarl ripped from him as he raced at the animal.

Glowing yellow eyes met his. The feral shifter made a keening sound, barreled right at him.

Madness gleamed in the animal's eyes.

Aldric was barely aware of anything as he ripped out the male's throat. The only things that existed were death and blood, the driving pain of grief and horror, as he tore the animal apart, limb from limb. Shredding the body until he was bathed in liquid crimson.

Red was everywhere, coating him as his wolf howled in agony.

The haze cleared for a moment. Looking around, he realized there was nothing left of the feral coyote. Entrails and other internal organs were strewn across the forest floor. Soon there would be nothing left of him at all.

Just as soon there would be nothing left of his dead mate and unborn child.

His child who'd never had the chance to take a breath, to open his eyes.

He couldn't look in that direction, couldn't look at what that beast had done. He and Isla might not have been bondmates, but they were mates and he loved her. When he thought of the terror, the pain of her final moments, a howl ripped from his throat as he tried to push the pain out of his body. Though he knew that would never happen.

He never should have left her alone. It was his fault she was gone, his unborn pup was gone. He should have protected them. He clawed at the ground, tossing up dirt and grass as he continued howling.

She'd been so tired when he'd left, had been insistent he go into the human village and get bread for her from the local baker. Isla had so many cravings over the course of her pregnancy, but he still shouldn't have left her.

He shouldn't have—

A familiar scent made him swivel toward the woods.

A scream of noise ripped through the air, angry and horrifying. He realized the sound was coming from him as all his rage and grief poured from his body. He was shaking. Nauseated, the pain of loss stealing the breath from his lungs.

Killing the feral animal who'd taken everything from him had done nothing to assuage the wrath that lived inside him.

Nothing would ever do that.

When he saw his brother loping toward him from the forest, his beast took over. He grasped at his animal, trying to wrest control away but it was too late...

Aldric's eyes popped open. Breathing hard, he stared at the ceiling. He forced himself to take a deep, calming breath.

Then another.

It had been a long damn time since he'd relived the familiar nightmare that wasn't a nightmare at all. The only thing he was grateful for was that he hadn't finished it. Because it always ended the same.

He tore his brother's face apart because he'd been in agony, and he'd lost everything. He'd not only lost his mate and unborn child, but severed the relationship with his brother until centuries later.

He rubbed a trembling hand over his face. His entire body was covered in a fine sheen of sweat. Still shaking, he sat up, cooling off as his heart rate returned to normal.

He wished it was nothing but an actual nightmare, not a memory he'd lived through.

A soft knocking at his bedroom door made him pause. He didn't think he'd cried out in his sleep. This place was insulated anyway.

After a glance at the clock he saw he'd only slept a few hours.

His eyes were gritty when he opened the door but when he saw Natalia standing there he straightened. If he'd been fully functioning, he would have scented her. But his senses were all screwed up after that nightmare.

Her dark hair was down around her shoulders in soft waves and she had on those same pajamas with the bicycles on them. They were so fucking adorable, so her. After the flashback he'd just had, he wanted to pull her into his arms.

"Is everything okay?" Her voice was low, the concern in her eyes palpable.

His first instinct was to say he was fine, but he didn't want to lie to her, didn't want to keep her out anymore. Now that he'd made the conscious choice to claim her, he knew he needed to let her into every part of his life. Even if she never reciprocated what he truly wanted, he still wouldn't regret being honest with her. "I... I had a nightmare." His voice was raspy.

Her eyes widened slightly and her scent gave away her surprise that he'd been honest. Without pause she stepped into his room and wrapped her arms around him in a hug.

Fuck him.

Even when she was angry with him, didn't trust him, didn't even want to be friends, she was still comforting him in a way he'd never let anyone. He'd been alone for so fucking long, had pushed everyone away because he hadn't thought he deserved any comfort. Somehow she'd sensed he needed her and now she was giving him the gift of her touch. His wolf needed soothing on the most basic level, and simple skin-to-skin contact was healing to all shifters. It didn't matter that she wasn't bare, this was what he needed.

She made him feel as if he wasn't alone anymore.

Breathing in her scent he wrapped his arms around her, buried his face against the top of her head as she laid her cheek against his chest. Her sweet cherry blossom scent filled his lungs and enveloped him, comforting him.

The secure way she held him made him want to never let go. He'd been craving this on every level. Deep down he worried that she'd think less of him if she knew the truth, knew how he'd failed the two wolves he was supposed to protect.

"You want to talk about it?" she whispered.

His heart cracked open even more. "Not right now." But he would later. He needed to tell her about his past, to fully let her in. Right now he simply wanted to hold her. Even if her touch was making his body flare to life in a way that would be hard to miss.

In response she rubbed his back in a sweet, soothing gesture. Her touch was a balm for his soul. This female was the perfect mix of sweetness and sass. If he'd wanted to come up with the fantasy woman for him, he never could have imagined someone like her. He would have fallen short.

She fit snugly against him, her petite body curving into his so that it would take nothing to hoist her up against the wall. His hands slid down her back and suddenly he wasn't just holding her because of a flashback, his hands were...on her ass. And there was no hiding his erection.

She froze.

At least she wasn't pushing him away. He couldn't help or hide his reaction to her. Not right now. Breathing erratically, she kept her face buried against his chest, her arms tight around him.

"I'm sorry," he managed to rasp out. Even though he wasn't sorry at all. He wanted this female more than his next breath, wanted to bury himself deep inside her, to share that intimate connection with her. But friends didn't get hard-ons for one another. And he was walking a tightrope with her, trying to build their friendship back before he even broached the subject of a relationship—of mating.

"It's okay." Clearing her throat, she took a step back but kept her hands on his waist.

Her touch made him want to rub up against her, beg for more. He wanted to feel her hands over every inch of him, teasing and caressing. Make him forget his horrific memories. Give him something pure and beautiful to focus on instead. Give him hope that he no longer had to roam the earth alone for the rest of his existence.

At the sound of a door being opened down the hallway, she released him as if she'd been burned and stepped back. Disappointment lanced through him, but he reined in the reaction. He didn't want her to feel guilty.

Aldric took a step into the entryway so he could see who it was. Immediately his gut dropped when he saw his brother's grim expression from down the hallway.

"Leigh Dawson has been murdered. The scent of a shifter is all over the crime scene."

Chapter 21

Aldric kept his voice low as he spoke to Ivonne. The female was in a state of shock, staring at Aldric blankly as he asked her questions.

Questions he hated even asking but he had a job to do. With two vampires missing and one now dead, this did not look good for the Kinley pack. And people had started to notice that Arthur and Darius were missing by this point. There was no more hiding the situation from either the Clifton coven or the Kinley pack. The vampire leader and pack Alpha were in the next room, waiting for Aldric to finish.

"How do you think someone got into your house?" he asked again when Ivonne didn't answer the first time.

Natalia sat next to Ivonne and placed a gentle hand over hers. The action seemed to pull Ivonne out of her catatonic state.

She cleared her throat. "I...I was with Crystal."

"She lives here?"

The female shook her head. "No. Leigh and I have—had—an open relationship." Her voice cracked on the last word. She swatted away tears. "I asked Crystal to stay today so we could..." She cleared her throat again. "Leigh didn't want to join us. My mate was alone, hurt, dying, and I was..." Her voice broke again and she buried her face in her hands, her shoulders shaking as she silently cried.

Aldric might not understand how anyone could have open relationships, but her grief was real. A plethora of emotions rolled off her, too many to sift through, but the grief stood out. An emotion he was intimately familiar with.

Natalia murmured soothing sounds and wrapped an arm around Ivonne's shoulders. She didn't tell her everything would be okay or spout stupid fucking platitudes. But she did give comfort, just as she had him a little while ago.

Natalia had lost too many of her own people recently. Her parents and two cousins had all been murdered. And he'd simply added to her pain when he'd left her with no word. God, he'd fucked up. No wonder she didn't want him in her life.

"I know this is difficult," he murmured. "And I'm sorry for your loss. Would you like me to call Elian in here?"

Shaking her head, she straightened and looked at him. "No, I want whoever hurt my mate to pay." Something he recognized well bled into her gaze. Rage. "A shifter murdered my mate. It had to be a Kinley shifter! They need to be brought to justice."

Aldric nodded, shooting a quick look at Natalia. She'd scented shifter in the bloody bedroom as well. They all had—Jayce, Kat and the two leaders. He recognized who the scent belonged to but he wasn't going to tell Ivonne that. She would immediately want blood, and if she didn't recognize it right now, it would keep the peace at least a little longer. Until they could figure this mess out.

Natalia's expression was worried too. He hadn't told her he knew that scent but she'd told him it was definitely a shifter. Lupine.

"I'm going to have to ask a lot of questions. Are you sure you don't want your coven leader in here?" If she'd been a shifter she would have asked for her Alpha as support. It was more or less the way things were done.

Another sharp shake of her head. "I'm sure. I need to get through this. I'll break down once we're done. My mate deserves justice." Her words were resolute.

Nodding, he dove right in, asking question after question. Who had access to their home, who knew about their open relationship, on and on.

"How far away is the room you were in earlier from your bedroom?"

"We have a playroom. It's only a floor down but it's well insulated. I..." Jaw tight, she seemed to steady herself. "It's locked both when in use and when it's not, so no one could have bothered us."

"Who else on the premises entered the bedroom after you found him?" He hated asking but he needed to know how contaminated the scene was.

Someone had driven a silver stake straight through Leigh's chest, piercing his heart. The killing blow. The silver would have injured him, but vampires and shifters couldn't live once their hearts were shredded. Not usually anyway. The male had been ripped apart, ripped to pieces by claws. But from what Aldric had seen, he hadn't struggled. There were no defensive wounds and the blows had been vicious. An autopsy would tell for certain, but he was sure that the male had been clawed up postmortem. That was odd.

"No one. I called Elian immediately after I found..."

"Were you and Crystal together the entire time in the playroom?"

She started to nod, but quickly shook her head. "No. She got blood for us after a couple hours because we were tired."

"Around what time was that?"

As she continued to answer questions, Aldric jotted down her answers. He had an excellent memory but keeping detailed notes was necessary for everyone involved in this case.

After twenty more minutes of questioning her, he met with Crystal while Natalia left to help Kat and Jayce search for scents on the property. Crystal's story lined up with Ivonne's, but didn't sound rehearsed.

Once he was done with her, he continued questioning the rest of the staff, the tediousness necessary, if time-consuming. It was more logical that someone inside the house or someone with access to Ivonne and Leigh's schedule had been involved.

Especially since Ivonne was certain that she'd armed their security system. He'd have to check the records, to see when it had been disabled.

What really mattered though, were the scents in the house. Because scents didn't lie. Not to shifters and vampires.

Scents couldn't be faked—not that he knew of anyway. And he had no doubt that Constance Kinley's scent was in that bedroom, all over Leigh's dead body.

Aldric nodded once at Craig Kinley as he exited the study. The Alpha's entire body was like a tightrope, all his muscles pulled taut. With a dark expression he fell into step with Aldric and headed down the hallway to the front door.

They stepped outside to find two shifters from the Kinley pack waiting, but Craig continued past them without a word. Aldric scented traces of Jayce, Kat and Natalia nearby. Scenting Natalia soothed his wolf. He liked having her near, wished she was with him now.

But she didn't need to be here for this conversation.

"You know what I scented in there," Aldric said as they moved into the middle of the expansive front yard. He wasn't going to spell it out, not with shifters and vampires in the near vicinity.

"I do. But it wasn't her." The Alpha's voice was tight, rage vibrating in his words.

Aldric didn't bother arguing because there was no point. "I'm going to need to talk to her. Now. Where is she?"

"It wasn't her," he growled, more animal than human.

"Then my talking to her won't change that." He kept his voice calm but didn't back down. One of the reasons he was so good at his job was because he was able to keep a level head, and he didn't have that compulsion to avert his eyes when dealing with Alphas. Jayce didn't either. They were both apex predators and even if neither of them wanted to run their own pack, they had Alpha blood.

"I won't let you take her," Craig growled, his canines descending.

Aldric allowed his wolf to show in his eyes, releasing his canines. "I talk to her now. Unless you want to go to war with not only the Clifton coven, but the Brethren. And probably The Council. Don't be fucking stupid."

The male struggled to contain his wolf for a long few moments before his canines retracted. He nodded. "You can speak to her. In my territory."

Aldric nodded. "I'm bringing my people with me. We'll need to confirm her scent."

The Alpha clearly wanted to slash out at Aldric, but he nodded. Because once they confirmed Constance's scent as the same fresh one from the crime scene, it would be a shit show.

And at this point Aldric didn't think there would be an issue confirming her scent. He knew what he'd smelled in there.

He had to bring the killer to justice if he wanted to stop a war from breaking out.

Chapter 22

Aldric nodded once at Craig, who stood by Constance in the Alpha's kitchen. Her scent was unmistakable. It reminded him of the desert at night, of sand and a blanket of stars across the sky. It was unique, as with all shifters.

The auburn-haired female stood with her legs spread a foot apart, her arms crossed over her chest as she stared in defiance at Aldric and Natalia. Jayce and Kat had already verified her scent and had left, going to hunt down another lead. "I don't give a shit if an entire squadron of trackers says my scent is at the Dawson house, I've never fucking been there." Her words were a snarl.

From what Aldric knew of her, the show of temper was rare. But she was being accused of murder. The penalty for which was death for their kind. If it was proved she was behind the murder of Leigh Dawson, she'd be executed. And if the Kinley Alpha refused to give her up to face her punishment, there would definitely be a war.

Blood would be shed and potentially hundreds would die.

"Maybe you weren't there, but your scent is." Natalia's voice was soft, calming. "Scenting out individuals is one of my gifts. Even your own father scented you there." There was no anger in her words, just truth.

Constance's jaw tightened, her body vibrating with rage. "My mate is missing and now someone's trying to frame me for murder. This is insanity," she rasped out.

"Why would someone want to frame you for murder?" Aldric asked, pulling out a seat at the kitchen island.

Natalia did the same.

Both Constance and Craig relaxed the slightest fraction. It wasn't so much their body language but the change in their scents. Though Craig was difficult to read completely since he was an Alpha. He had to be more than worried about his daughter.

"The peace treaty seems like the most obvious reason. There are a few females in Darius's coven who would likely want to shred me to ribbons if they knew I was about to mate with him. But killing me or framing me won't get them him. He loves me."

Aldric knew logic didn't often come into play with matters of the heart. Especially if a narcissistic, crazy vampire wanted Darius and couldn't have him. Getting rid of Constance would be all that mattered to her. But...it seemed off for what had happened so far. Two vampire males were missing and now one had been murdered. And what, all to frame Constance? When killing her would have been an easier option? Not that he thought killing the female would be easy, but it made more sense than framing her. This felt personal.

"Let's say I believe you're innocent." Because Aldric didn't think this female had killed Leigh Dawson.

He knew that some individuals could cover up the scent of their lies. It was extremely difficult, but not an impossibility. Sociopaths didn't give off a scent when they lied, and others with inborn gifts, usually Alphas, could actually cover certain scents.

From Constance's reputation, she wouldn't hide killing someone. She'd come out and do it so everyone knew. She didn't seem like a coward. And killing this vampire would only hurt her relationship with her almost-mate. There was no motive.

Her eyes went golden lupine. "I *am* innocent!"

He continued. "You're going to have to stay on lockdown here at your Alpha's home while we find out who's behind Dawson's murder. And," he added, looking at Craig, "you'll have to agree to keep two of Elian's representatives here as well at all times. If this is the beginning of something bigger, she has to be under surveillance 24/7." If there were future murders, it would prove she wasn't behind them. And it would keep the vampires relatively calm that their number one suspect wasn't trying to escape the country.

Constance opened her mouth, clearly to argue, but her Alpha held up a hand. He looked at Aldric for a long moment, assessing him with eyes turned that same familial golden lupine. Finally he nodded. "I agree to this."

Aldric hadn't doubted the male would. This was beyond fair. "I've already discussed my terms with Elian, of keeping Constance locked down here. He's agreed." Aldric had called the vampire leader and gone over everything with him on the drive here. He'd needed to make sure Elian was on board with this. Because the male had every right to insist that Constance be kept prisoner in his own territory.

Craig's brow furrowed ever so slightly, clearly surprised the male had agreed to the terms.

Aldric was always objective in his investigations but he could admit that he didn't want these two factions to go to war. It would be shitty for everyone, could affect many other packs and the supernaturals' relationship with humans. There would be no winners. So he added, "He told me that if he's going to sign a treaty with you, he would trust you with this. Trust you not to betray his coven, *him*." Because if Craig did betray the vampires, there was no going back for the pack and the coven. There would be no peace. Elian was making a big concession by allowing Constance to remain in her pack's territory while she was a murder suspect.

Craig only nodded. After speaking to Constance for another fifteen minutes, Aldric and Natalia left.

"The Alpha, he won't hand his daughter over for death," Natalia said quietly as Aldric steered out of the driveway. The pack's land was different than the vampires. It was more similar to where Natalia lived, out in the country with a big spread of houses and cabins so that the pack was all close together. "Even if it goes against his honor code, and even if he doesn't want to betray the trust of Elian...he'll do whatever it takes to keep her alive. He's her *father*."

Aldric nodded, knowing it was pure truth. "Let's find out who the fuck is behind all this, then."

Once this investigation was over all his focus was going to be on Natalia. He wouldn't rest until she was his. She already owned him even if she didn't realize it.

Chapter 23

"Omari and Cyrus don't know you're coming, but they will let you into their home." Elian's biting voice came over the phone line. Aldric had the coven leader on speaker, wanted Natalia to hear everything clearly. "If they don't, contact me."

Aldric wouldn't bother, he'd just incapacitate the two males, but he kept his voice civil. "I will. Thank you for being so accommodating with the Constance situation."

The polished male cursed. "I truly don't think she did this but her scent..."

The male didn't need to finish. In the end it wouldn't matter what even the coven leader thought. The evidence was all that mattered. And Elian's coven would demand blood once it was determined the shifter female was behind the murder. He could let her go, declare her innocent, but it still wouldn't matter. The peace treaty wouldn't go through and there would continue to be bad blood between the two factions until more blood was spilled.

After they disconnected, Natalia said, "So who are these two males we're going to talk to? They weren't on our list of suspects."

"I overheard them talking at the party the other night. Their topic of conversation was masking scents and duplicating them."

Natalia's eyebrows raised. "Interesting conversation."

"They haven't been part of the coven long enough to have any ill will toward the Kinley pack, which is why they weren't on the list." And their conversation could be nothing, but after this murder and a suspect he didn't think was guilty, these two males were getting an unexpected visit from him. Aldric just hoped Elian was telling him the truth, that they truly didn't know of his arrival. Questioning a suspect when they weren't expecting him made it easier to gauge the truth from people.

"Are they mates?"

Aldric nodded. "And they don't have an open relationship."

"Rare for vampires apparently." Her voice was dry.

No kidding.

It didn't take long to reach the mated pair's home. Much like the rest of the coven, these two had a monstrous residence as well.

Aldric had his weapons visibly strapped to his thighs, wanting these males to know exactly why he was here. After they rang the doorbell, the door opened almost two full minutes later to reveal both men, impeccably dressed in dark slacks and different colored cashmere sweaters—but their faces were flushed and the scent of mating was thick in the air.

Omari, the older male by about two years, stood half in front of Cyrus, his body language protective. "Yes?" His accent was faint, but even if Aldric didn't have a very thin file on the male, he would have known he was from Egypt after having spent a decade there.

"We need to speak with you."

The male lifted an eyebrow. "About?"

"Murder."

Without blinking, Omari stepped back, still half-blocking Cyrus who simply sighed. "You're working for our Brethren." Not a question.

Who he was, was common knowledge and by now the coven and pack all knew why he was here. "I overheard you talking the other night about masking scents and duplicating scents. I also know that you," he said to Cyrus, "have a chemistry background."

The male with the olive skin gave a half-nod. "I do."

"And I have multiple degrees in biology. What do you want with us?" Omari demanded. He crossed his arms over his broad chest.

"One of your coven members was murdered tonight," Natalia said quietly.

They both looked at her, the surprise that rolled off both of them real even if their expressions didn't change much.

Omari spoke again, clearly the alpha of the relationship. "Who? How? Ah... Do you want to come in and sit?"

Aldric ignored the questions. "What are your thoughts on the peace treaty?"

Both men shrugged. "It is a good thing," Omari said as Cyrus nodded, nudging his mate aside so he could stand next to him.

"We have friends within the Kinley pack, as do many of the newer coven members. We joined with Elian because of his reputation as a fair leader, but we don't want to go to war with anyone."

Aldric had heard much the same from other newer coven members. "Why were you talking about masking scents or duplicating scents?"

Both men blinked at him.

This time Cyrus spoke first. "Why wouldn't we? It's fascinating to think we will get there one day."

"One day?" Natalia asked.

The male nodded. "Shifters and vampires have such acute senses, it's pretty much impossible to fake scents. The thought of being able to truly duplicate something, an inborn scent of say, a vampire... it's fascinating." His green eyes glowed slightly at the thought.

Aldric didn't think it was fascinating so much as terrifying. Being able to distinguish various scents was part of what helped their kind to survive. He needed to be able to trust his senses. All shifters did. His wolf's hackles raised at the thought of not being able to trust that intrinsic part of him. "Are either of you working on a project related to modulating scents?" Aldric had learned from Elian that both males had labs, worked independently on various things he wouldn't understand. They each had various patents as well.

"No, but what is this about?" Omari demanded.

The news of Leigh's death would spread to the rest of the coven and likely the Kinley pack in a few hours. Of that, Aldric had no doubt. There was no reason to hold back information the two males would soon find out. "Is there somewhere we can sit and speak?"

Omari nodded. "This way. We don't have any staff on site currently but if you'd like refreshments—"

"We're okay." They needed to talk so he and Natalia could get out of here. The clock was ticking down and they needed to find whoever had murdered Leigh Dawson.

After a lengthy conversation with the two males, Natalia and Aldric let Omari escort them to the front door.

As they were leaving, Omari said, "Truly, the only tried and true way to make sure a person's scent is somewhere they're not is to use that person's clothing or belongings. But it should be something they've worn on their body."

Aldric simply nodded politely, because yeah, he'd already thought of that. So had Natalia.

Once in the truck, Natalia let out a growl of frustration. "That was freaking pointless."

He shoved out a breath, as frustrated as she was.

She turned to look at him as he steered out of the driveway. "You think they were lying?"

"No, and I believed them when they said the science for duplicating scents isn't there yet."

"Thank God. How messed up would that be?"

He didn't even want to imagine.

"I feel like we're back to square one," she muttered, looking out the passenger window as they headed down the street.

"At least we've eliminated two potential suspects." He had to look at any investigations like that. And his gut told him those two males weren't involved.

"Still frustrating," she grumbled.

He started to remind her that once upon a time she'd begged to come on investigations with him. Before the words could form, he clenched his jaw shut tight. Oh yeah, reminding her of the way he'd fucked up, of the last time she'd asked him to go on a hunt and he'd shut her down, would be real smart.

Against his will, in his head he replayed that last day he'd seen her. He'd only meant to get some distance from her, not cut and run completely. But after that morning, after he'd been ready to take her right up against the front door of her home, he'd run like a coward.

Rolling his shoulders once, he tried to lock up the memory but it was no use.

He stood outside the home Natalia shared with her sisters, stared at his phone for a long moment. He didn't want to want her as much as he did, but he craved being around her.

Which was why he'd agreed to this recent job from the Brethren. A simple bounty hunting thing, but it would take him away from here. From her.

He needed space from her for his sanity.

But he also had to tell her he was leaving, even if it was close to dawn. Trying not to think about what she looked like upstairs in her bed, her sheets all tangled around her, he texted her. Downstairs, didn't want to knock and wake everyone. Can you come down?

Be right down.

A couple minutes later she stepped outside wearing long-sleeved pink and black pajamas. When she stepped onto the porch, his breath caught in his throat as it always did around her. A faint minty scent teased the air, telling him she'd brushed her teeth.

She smiled at him, the sight a kick to his senses, but it faded as her gaze landed on his duffel bag. "Is everything okay?" She pulled the door shut behind her.

A cool breeze kicked up but he barely felt it, not for the heat humming through his blood as he watched the petite female who'd come to mean way too much to him in recent months.

He rubbed a hand over his buzz cut, nodded, even as he ignored the way her eyes tracked the muscles of his forearm. He cleared his throat. "Yeah, got called away for a bounty hunting job. Last minute thing and the money's good." Truth was, he didn't need the money, even if it was a nice paycheck.

Disappointment flickered in her espresso eyes. "How long will you be gone?"

He was far too pleased that she cared he was leaving. Part of him wanted to ask her to come with him, knew she would if he asked. He lifted a shoulder instead. "Week, probably. Two at the most. The Brethren hired me for this one."

"Take me with you."

Despite the spring month, another cold breeze kicked up. His wolf snarled at him, telling him to say yes, but he forced his expression to remain neutral. His hunger for Natalia was growing every day, with a vengeance he couldn't control. "I...can't."

Now pure hurt filled her expression as she wrapped her arms around herself. "Why not?"

"It's too dangerous." Words that weren't exactly a lie, since the mission was dangerous. But he could still take her. He couldn't bring her with him on another mission, however, for a totally different reason. He no longer trusted himself around her.

"I'm a shifter, I can take care of myself." Heat laced her words. "Come on, you know we'll have fun together." Smiling, she stepped closer to him, the grin on her lips hinting at flirting.

Her scent wrapped around him, made him lightheaded for a moment. "No." He tightened his jaw, solidifying his resolve. "I just came by to tell you, but I can't waste any more time." Liar, liar, *his wolf snarled.*

She stilled, hurt bleeding into her dark gaze. "You've taken me in the past. Is this job different?" Her voice sounded small.

He knew his wolf was in his gaze as he watched her. He wanted to pin her up against the door, to take her right up on it, to claim and mark her so every-fuck-ing-one knew she was his.

"Aldric?" Her brief touch on his forearm had him moving before he realized his intentions.

He pressed her against the door, inhaling deeply, her cherry blossom and vanilla scent making him crazed. His wolf clawed at him, sharper and deeper this time, demanding.

She gasped once but arched into him as if it was the most natural thing in the world.

The feel of the sensual female moving against him, practically purring, was too much. She was so sweet—definitely not for him. He needed to stay away.

Hell, to run away. Before they both got burned to ashes. Because this wouldn't end well. He'd screw up and hurt her. He'd let down the one female he'd been meant to protect, and Natalia already meant more to him than... He shoved the thought away and bent his head down to her neck. He ran his nose along the elegant column and inhaled again.

Mine.

His fingers curled against the wood of the door on either side of her head. He liked caging her in, liked having her so damn close. "I let you boss me around occasionally because I find it sexy and charming," he growled.

Not exactly a lie either. He did find it hot when she bossed him around. But when it came to anything sexual, he needed to be in charge and right now she was pushing him.

He ran his nose along her jaw and throat, moving to the other side of her neck. The compulsion to scent all of her was overwhelming. "But I won't explain myself further about this job. So don't think you can use your charms to get what you want. Don't. Push. Me." If she did, he was certain he wouldn't be able to hold back any longer.

Her breathing was as erratic as his, the scent of her desire an aphrodisiac that nothing could ever compare to.

Instead of shoving him back, she reached up and tentatively trailed her fingers down his chest. He wished he could feel those fingers on his skin.

A shudder racked him and he buried his face against her neck. Groaning, he did the one thing he shouldn't. He scraped his canines against her neck, something he had no right to do. His control was slipping, fast and frantic.

Another, more potent scent rolled off her, pure sex and sin. She wanted him as much as he wanted her. There was no doubt in his mind.

No, no, no.

His claws extended without thought, digging into the door. Before, he'd been uncertain what she wanted, if she even wanted him at all. To scent her desire so pure, so strong... He shoved back, grabbed his bag and left.

He had to get far, far away from her before he did something they'd both regret.

Chapter 24

Things were going better than she'd planned. In the last couple hours the knowledge of a Clifton vampire murder at the hands of a Kinley shifter had spread like a plague throughout the coven.

Leigh hadn't been extremely well-liked, but he was still a vampire. One of them. Not a fucking animal.

So far no names had been given about who the guilty party was, but she had no doubt that would come soon enough. Eventually one of those shifters would figure out Constance's scent was all over the crime scene. And Elian had to know as well—he should be the one announcing the new info to his own coven but for some reason was sitting on it. The knowledge pissed her off. But things would fall into place, she just had to be patient. With the set-up murder scene, it would be easy for the coven to convict that bitch and sentence her to death.

If Constance's pack didn't turn the shifter over, well, she had a backup plan for that scenario. It would require testing how much the shifter female truly loved Darius.

Threatening to kill her almost-mate unless Constance turned herself in—that would get tricky, so she'd have to make sure to pressure Constance that if the shifter female told anyone that Darius was still alive, he would die immediately. That *should* be good enough motivation for the bitch to turn herself over to the Clifton coven.

She wanted to strike while news of the murder was still spreading throughout her coven. So she made a phone call. Then another.

Feeding the fire of old grudges against the Kinley pack was harder than she'd thought. It seemed that her people really did want peace. They were sympathetic to Leigh's death, of course, but there hadn't been calls for vengeance as she'd assumed. She'd only spoken to the newer generation and the newer members, however. Their lack of demand for justice rankled her to her core. Vampires were predators. Peace wasn't a way of life. She sneered at the thought. God, her people were turning into shadows of what they'd once been.

The older generation, her generation, would be easier to sway. They remembered the wars between the shifters, the blood and death. Changing tactics, she started contacting the older guard.

She didn't care if there was peace or war. She was old enough to know that things never stayed the same. Even if there was peace for a time, war would come soon enough. Whether from the Kinley pack or another threat, there would always be war. Part of her missed the constant fighting. It was her predatory nature, her lust for blood.

Right now all she wanted was vengeance—for Constance to die and Craig to suffer. And she would have the revenge she deserved. It was the only way she could go to her grave in peace, to be certain that fucking Alpha paid for his crimes.

Thinking about the agony he would be in, the rage and helplessness he would feel, a surge of hunger spiraled through her body. Her breasts grew heavy and heat flooded between her thighs.

She desperately wished she had someone to help her with release, but that wasn't possible now. When she'd first come up with the idea to capture Darius she'd toyed with the idea of chaining him up and fucking him. Sending pictures of Darius with another female to Constance would have been brilliant. God, the pain it would have caused the other female would have made this plan even better.

She stroked between her thighs at the thought of forcing that stupid, traitorous vampire to get hard, to fuck him against his will, to bring her pleasure against his will. He deserved everything that happened to him for taking up with an animal.

But there were too many risks. Even chained and restrained there was no guarantee she'd be able to get Darius hard. And on the chance that she did, she wouldn't risk him escaping his chains and hurting her. In the cage the male was subdued because of the spell she'd had a witch cast around it. Chains were a different story.

Nonetheless, things were still going according to plan.

She began stroking herself harder, rubbing her already pulsing clit as she relished all the pain and suffering she was causing.

This revenge had been years in the making. Now that it was finally here, she could hardly believe it.

Chapter 25

Natalia stripped off her scarf and hat as she and Aldric stepped back into the B&B. A light blanket of snow covered everything outside and the icy chill in the air followed them into the foyer even after the door was shut.

She knew that they were the first ones back, since Jayce had texted Aldric that he and Kat were running down a lead on an enemy of the deceased Leigh Dawson, who'd recently done some business transactions with the dead male. Things had gone south, and with Leigh out of the way, it would be a very good turn of events for the vampire he'd been working with.

They didn't have any proof the male was involved but it would be stupid not to at least talk to the guy.

Her phone dinged with an incoming text as Aldric shut the door behind them. *Sent you a few more files on Ivonne and Crystal. Unfortunately not much available.* It was from her packmate, Ryan, hacker extraordinaire. He was also her brother-in-law since he'd recently mated with her oldest sister.

"Ryan sent us something about Ivonne and Crystal. I should have known he'd be up even at one in the morning," she said as they headed into the study, which they'd turned into their command center, complete with a big whiteboard. Anyone who was a suspect was on that board.

The owner of the B&B was apparently above reproach, according to Jayce, and kept this place locked down tight when they weren't here. Natalia knew that jaguars preferred to live alone or in small packs but wondered if it was hard for the female to run this place by herself. Shifters tended to need touch. Natalia couldn't imagine not living with a pack or other shifters.

Jayce had told Natalia that the female had not only video cameras and a top-of-the-line security system, but she employed supernatural methods of security as well in the form of spells. So if any of her alarms went off she'd know immediately. The spells freaked Natalia out a little because it was very different than the natural magic that let her shift into her wolf.

Natalia's gaze landed on Ivonne's picture on the board. "I know vampires are different but I don't get being okay with sharing your mate," she murmured.

"If you were mine, I would never share you." Aldric's deeply spoken words came out guttural.

She swiveled to find him watching her with grayish-green eyes gone lupine. The truth of his statement wrapped around her, the possession in his voice making heat shimmer through her. Too much was between them. He'd hurt her so badly. But being around him for this investigation desperately made her want to reconsider what she'd said to him.

Because she did want the male in her life. "I..." She wanted to tell him that she could never come second to a dead mate, never wanted to be compared to someone else. But she wasn't sure how seriously to take him. She believed he meant what he said but he'd also made it crystal freaking clear that he just wanted friendship from her. She couldn't do just friendship, even if she wanted to try. It would hurt too much.

Instead of continuing, she turned back to the board. It was definitely time for a subject change.

"I hate saying this, but something about Ivonne bothered me. Which is stupid, because there's no rulebook for grief. God, she lost her mate. That's gotta be—" She winced, feeling like a jerk. Of course Aldric knew how hard it was.

He moved to stand next to her, his presence impossible to ignore. "Finding my mate, finding Isla's broken body..." His voice cracked. "It was the hardest fucking thing in the world."

Natalia went motionless. For so damn long she'd wanted him to open up. She wanted to know what had happened to his mate. Not out of morbid curiosity, but because she wanted to know everything about him, for him to trust her enough to be real, be honest about what had to have been the most altering event of his very long life. Instead of responding, she went on instinct and reached for his hand, grasping his much bigger one in hers.

From the riot of emotions rolling off him she knew that his wolf needed touch.

He squeezed once, but didn't look at her. Just stared at the whiteboard of names and faces. He wasn't really seeing anything though, that much she could tell. His eyes had glazed over and she wondered what he was remembering.

"I found them. Found Isla. She was dead by the time I got there, her body ravaged. My..." He cleared his throat, his voice thick with grief. "It was a feral coyote. I killed him immediately. Went into a blind rage. Afterward I lost complete control. I attacked my brother in my pain, then ran. I roamed for so fucking long." The words poured from him as if he couldn't stop himself.

She didn't want him to stop.

"For decades I stayed in wolf form, just roaming. It's a miracle I didn't go feral myself." Now he looked at her, his eyes human again. Too many emotions flickered in his gaze—sadness, regret, others she couldn't even define. "She was pregnant when she died, and something inside me snapped when I saw what that coyote had done. It took a long time to become human again, to start living again. And the truth is, I don't know how well I've been living the past couple centuries anyway. I've been a fucking shadow of a wolf—until you."

A wealth of emotions flooded Natalia as she digested his words, as his own emotions rolled over her in a tidal wave. He was saying things she'd needed to hear, but the pain in his voice shredded her up.

"I never bonded with her. We were mates, not bondmates."

Natalia blinked, surprised at the admission itself and the truth of his words. She'd assumed they'd been bondmates by the way he'd seemed to grieve for so long. He was so damn alpha. Bondmates were linked for life, unable to leave each other. "I don't know what to say to that."

His jaw clenched tight. "I'm not... diminishing what I had with Isla. I did love her. But it wasn't all-consuming. We were mated because it was simply what lupines did back then. I didn't know any other she-wolves in the area and we fit. She was sweet and submissive. She never pushed for a bondmating either."

A pang of... Natalia wasn't sure what she was feeling. Jealousy? She felt like shit at hearing his description of his dead mate. She couldn't be jealous of someone long gone. Yet, she kind of was.

He didn't seem to notice her inner turmoil as he continued. "The nature of her death tore me up and..." He scrubbed a hand over his face, the sharp scent of guilt pouring off him so starkly it was suffocating. "I've never admitted this out loud, never wanted to. I felt guilty because I wasn't there to protect her, and because I should have loved her more." Now in addition to guilt she sensed shame coming off him. "I see what my brother has with Kat, and..." He shook his head, turned away from her.

Natalia wasn't sure what to say, if she should say *anything*. When he didn't make a move to leave the room, just kept his back to her, his body rigidly tight, she wrapped her arms around him from behind. There was simply no way she could just ignore his pain, *not* comfort him. Like the time he'd told her that he hadn't celebrated Christmas in centuries. It had made her want to pull him into her arms and hug away his pain.

The agony and shame coming from him tore her up. She laid her cheek against his back. His big body vibrated, tensed for a moment before he let out a shuddering breath.

"I'm sorry for the way I hurt you." His words were savage, real. A dark truth. "You're the last person on the fucking planet I'd ever want to hurt. The first time I met you, I felt a spark of something... Something I don't ever remember having. When you told me you would flay me alive if I didn't let you out of that elevator, I got more turned on than I've ever been in my life."

She snorted against his back, even if she'd felt the same way the night they'd met. It didn't matter that she'd wanted to smack the obnoxious look off his face. Her wolf had recognized something in him on a primal level that she hadn't been able to admit until much later. "You're such a liar."

He turned to face her and not for the first time she thought of how small he made her feel. She was petite anyway, but he was huge, even by shifter standards. Without trying he made her feel feminine and protected.

"You made me feel alive, Natalia. Ever since that day I've been fighting what I feel for you."

Looking up into eyes once again turned lupine, her own wolf responded to the pull she felt to this male. She leaned into his embrace as a rush of heat flooded between her thighs. There was no hiding her reaction to him. Even if she'd wanted to try, she simply couldn't.

Everything he'd just admitted was... Hell, she didn't know what to do with the overload of information. He'd opened up to her in a way she'd dreamed about for so long. She needed so badly to hope that maybe, just maybe, he was saying he wanted more with her, that there could be something real between them, something more than friendship. But she was too afraid to ask the words, too afraid of the rejection that might follow. He was speaking the truth but she still sensed the shame and guilt from the way he seemed to think he'd failed his mate.

Right now, Natalia didn't even want to think about that, didn't want to let her own feelings of someone long gone cloud her mind. Letting her wolf take over, she lifted up on her tiptoes. Before she'd moved even a few inches Aldric's mouth crushed over hers.

Demanding, hungry, consuming.

His tongue invaded her mouth, tasting and teasing. A growl rumbled in his throat and she couldn't help her own groaning response.

Her most primal side was taking over in a way that had never happened. She didn't care where they were, she just knew she wanted to claim this male. She wasn't sure what the hell was going on, what the future held or if he'd regret this kiss as soon as it was over, so for now, she held on tight.

She fisted her hands in his shirt, clutching the material and his shoulders. She was vaguely aware of moving backward. When her back connected with a wall, her eyes flew open.

Aldric looked down at her, the purest hunger in his gaze. Her throat seized as she stared up at him. Everything around them fell away as he hoisted her up. Without thought, she wrapped her legs around him. What she wouldn't give to feel him—

A door slammed.

She blinked even as Aldric snarled and turned. She dropped her legs, returning to the floor as he swiveled fully, moving his body in front of her to shield her from... Niko's scent trickled through the haze of lust filling the air.

"Shit," she heard him mutter because she couldn't see him around Aldric's huge frame. "I'll come back."

"It's okay." Natalia squeezed Aldric's waist, stepped out from behind him. While she desperately wanted to follow through on what they'd just started, sanity was slowly returning. Because deep down, she kept waiting for him to do the same thing he'd done before. To cut and run.

They needed to talk more before things went any further. And she had no doubt that things would have definitely gone further without that interruption. She hadn't cared about anything other than feeling Aldric skin to skin, feeling him push deep inside her.

But she wouldn't be a mistake or a regret to him. No way. Her heart couldn't take it. She didn't think he would intentionally hurt her, but that wouldn't matter if he regretted something happening between them and then ran again. It would slice her up all the same. She'd already lost so many people in her life. She didn't want to fall even harder for him only to have him leave again.

Straightening her clothes, she nodded at Niko, who looked as if he was deciding if he should stay or go. Aldric simply watched the vampire with pure death in his gaze.

Clearing her throat, she tugged on Aldric's arm. Blinking, he focused on her. "We need to work," she said. "We need to find out who killed Dawson."

He looked as if he wanted to argue, but nodded, his jaw tight. "This isn't over," he rasped out at a subvocal level she was certain even Niko couldn't hear. His words were just for her.

Yeah, she hadn't thought it would be. Everything else aside, she simply couldn't come second to a dead woman. A woman who was apparently sweet and submissive.

Nothing at all like Natalia.

The thought was a slap of ice water in her face. She turned away from him, stepped a couple feet away toward the whiteboard. "You find out anything useful tonight?" she asked Niko.

Aldric moved with her, placed a possessive hand at the back of her neck. The action was so unexpected she nearly jumped from the contact. When she looked up at him, his expression dared her to pull away.

Liking the feel of him touching her so possessively and unable to deny her hunger for that contact, she stepped a few inches closer. Her emotions were running haywire but she simply couldn't pull away from him, not now. The way he was holding her soothed all the jagged edges inside her. Even if she was terrified of the future between them, if there would ever even *be* one, she couldn't force her feet to move away. Because when he touched her like this, it felt right.

"I just left Ferguson's club. He's been there all night. I don't think he's involved in this," Niko said, keeping distance between them as he stood in the entryway of the study.

Before either of them could respond the front door opened again. Natalia scented Jayce and Kat before they appeared in the entryway next to Niko.

Jayce's gaze immediately went to Aldric's hand still set possessively on Natalia, but he didn't comment as he stalked into the room.

"What's going on?" Niko asked at the same time Aldric said, "What is it?"

"Word's already spread throughout the Clifton coven about Leigh's murder. Every home we stopped at already knew about Leigh's death. I knew word would spread, but now the vampires are talking about Darius and Arthur's disappearances. And...somehow they know it's Constance's scent at the house."

"Who recognized it?" Natalia asked. Because there hadn't been that many people at the crime scene.

"I don't know." Jayce's jaw tightened as Kat leaned against the entryway frame, her arms crossed over her chest.

"Now that Ivonne knows whose scent is at her home, she's demanding blood. She says her mate's death won't go unpunished. She's demanding an immediate execution." Kat's voice was tight.

Niko snorted. "Ivonne doesn't give a shit about Leigh." He said the words offhandedly. "The only person she ever cared about was her first mate."

The room went quiet as everyone turned to look at him.

He lifted an eyebrow. "What?"

Aldric tensed next to Natalia, but didn't drop his hand. His thumb was idly brushing against her neck. "She was mated before?"

Natalia frowned, desperately trying to ignore the pleasurable sensations coursing through her at Aldric's touch. That tidbit hadn't been in their file on Ivonne. It hadn't even been in the info Ryan had sent them.

Niko nodded. "Yeah. Few hundred years ago. She just married Leigh because of his wealth. She never got over the death of her first mate—who was a poor fool who couldn't keep any of his money. Gambling problem, I believe. And those two did *not* have an open relationship. She was wildly jealous of him, as he was of her. Their relationship was... toxic at best. But they stayed true to each other. I assumed you guys knew that."

"It's not in the file on her," Aldric said.

"It probably wouldn't be, considering vamp records. I'm not sure how he died. One of his gambling debts, maybe?" Niko lifted a shoulder. "It was so long ago and I'm not tight with anyone from this coven. I just remember she lost her mate, then later when she got mated again, many in the coven whispered about the reason behind her mating, considering she didn't stay faithful to Leigh."

"We need to talk to Ivonne again." Aldric's voice was tight. "Her mate was killed in their bed and didn't put up a fight. All those claw marks were post-mortem. According to the security records, the security system was turned off by someone inside the home..." He looked at Natalia and she could tell he was going to ask her to stay put. There was something about the look in his eyes.

She snorted. "I'm going."

"Aldric and I will take point with Ivonne," Jayce said, no room for argument in his voice. "You, Kat and Niko will stand guard around her home in case she tries to flee."

Natalia nodded, as did Kat. Even if she'd wanted to argue there was no point.

Not with these two alphas in charge. And the truth was, Ivonne was old and likely more powerful than Natalia and Kat. Probably not Niko, but still, it would be smarter to let Jayce and Aldric go into her home and subdue her if necessary. Maybe Ivonne had nothing to do with her mate's murder, but his death was so damn suspect.

Natalia couldn't imagine killing a mate, or killing anyone other than in self-defense. What if Ivonne had killed her first mate and now her second mate? She could have wanted to make it look like someone else did it, tried to frame Constance. Okay, maybe that was a bit of a stretch, even in her own mind, because she couldn't figure how it tied into Darius and Arthur's disappearances. Gah, this investigation was frustrating.

Aldric leaned down, brushed his mouth against her ear, jerking her from her thoughts. "When this is over, you're mine." His voice was a mere whisper but she felt the words all the way to her core.

A shiver racked through her. She wasn't sure what to do with what he'd just said. She wanted him, had for so damn long. But...his words could mean any number of things. He just said she was his, which could mean he wanted sex or a mating. He hadn't even bonded with his dead mate. And Natalia wouldn't settle for anything less. It was the way she was wired. When she committed to a mate it was going to be forever.

Chapter 26

Aldric moved quietly down one of the hallways in Ivonne's home. His claws were extended. Tonight he wouldn't bother with any other weapon. Ivonne might be older than him and Jayce but they were powerful and trained. Unlike his brother, he preferred to go wolf when he was fighting, rather than use blades.

There were too many scents in the house to get a pinpoint on her. The place was huge and it naturally smelled like her, her scent having infiltrated every facet of the home. The scent of death still lingered in the air as well. It was subtle but it seemed to stick to the walls. He still wasn't certain how Constance's scent had ended up here if she'd never been in the house. It was a mystery he planned to solve.

Ivonne hadn't responded to a call from either Jayce or her coven leader. Which could mean nothing, but they weren't taking chances. The fact that she hadn't responded to a call from Elian wasn't exactly suspect, but after just losing her mate, she should be available to her leader. Combined with what they'd just learned about her, Aldric wanted to make sure she was located. If she was the one behind her mate's death, she wouldn't blink at hurting anyone else. That bond was supposed to be sacrosanct. Even if she hadn't loved Leigh, they'd still been mates. Aldric wouldn't allow her to hurt someone else on his watch.

Part of Aldric didn't want her to be guilty, didn't want to think that someone could have killed their own mate. Even if he knew it did happen.

He didn't want to be here at all. He wanted to finish what he'd started with Natalia at the B&B. She'd tried to pull away from him when they'd been interrupted but something primitive inside him had refused to let her.

It didn't matter that he'd told himself to go slow, that he'd planned to rebuild their friendship first—and he still planned to do that—he hadn't been able to keep his hands off her. He'd needed to make it clear to Niko and any other male, including his happily mated brother, that Natalia was off-limits.

To everyone.

She shouldn't even be here, but he'd learned that trying to argue with her, especially when she and Kat were together, was a fruitless effort. Still...if Ivonne was a murdering psychopath, he didn't want Natalia anywhere near her. Which was why he'd been insistent she stay outside with Kat and Niko. He and Jayce could take care of one vampire.

Just like Natalia, Aldric had been bothered by Ivonne's reaction. He hadn't been able to put his finger on it, but his senses had been on high alert when questioning her. Natalia was right—there was no rulebook for grief. Even so, her reaction had been almost too perfect, as if it was scripted. Of course he could just be reading into things because he didn't particularly like the female. He tried to stay objective, was very good at it for the most part. However, he could admit that there were things he might never be objective about.

Her grief had been real when she'd talked about her mate though. He ran over the conversation they'd had with her and realized she'd never said Leigh's name. Just "my mate." An effective way to cover up her true feelings about her current mate, if she'd been intending to lie to them.

There were only a few hours until sunrise so if she had left the premises, she wouldn't have gone far. Before he'd left her home earlier she'd been insistent that she would stay here because it made her feel closer to her mate.

That was one thing Aldric didn't understand. He wouldn't have been able to stay under the same roof where his mate had been murdered.

Ivonne had said she didn't want to be around anyone else, wanted to grieve in peace and be near her "heart." Fucking bullshit.

When he heard a faint heartbeat a few doors down, he slowed until he reached the wall directly outside it.

Jayce was on the first floor, doing his own sweep, so it wasn't him.

Listening carefully, he heard only a shuffling. Dim light streamed through the half-opened doorway.

Retracting his claws, he gently pushed the door open a few inches more so he could slip inside.

With her back to him, one of the females he'd interviewed at the house before was packing a small black canvas Chanel bag. He recognized it from Ivonne's closet when he'd swept the crime scene earlier.

"What are you doing?"

The blonde jumped, swiveled to face him with wide green eyes. She had a similar look to Ivonne, tall and willowy. Just like Crystal, the other female Ivonne seemed to like fucking. It was a little strange how she liked to sleep with females who looked so much like her. This one...Hilary, was much younger than the other two. He knew that not only from her file, but by the low-level amount of power she radiated.

She looked around, panic in her gaze, before settling back on him. "I should ask you that," she snapped, her voice trembling.

He tilted his head slightly to the side, not responding as he let his claws extend.

Fear rolled off her in sickening waves as she watched him. With some beings he didn't have to use any sort of violence to get the answers he wanted. Sometimes the threat of it was enough. After interviewing Ivonne, Crystal and a whole host of others, this female included, he'd noticed that most in this household were afraid of shifters.

"I'm just packing a bag," Hilary finally said into the tense silence. "That's not a crime!"

"Didn't say it was." He stalked toward her in a way he knew would frighten her. "Where's Ivonne?" He eyed the contents of her bag. Not clothes, but various knickknacks from around the house. Some he recognized from the last time they'd been here just hours ago.

She shrugged jerkily, her body trembling. She didn't step back from him, he'd give her that. Even shaking, she stood her ground next to the end of the bed. "She said I could take this stuff."

An acidic stench filled the air.

He lifted an eyebrow at the evidence of a lie.

"Fine! But I'm not going down for that bitch. She doesn't know that I know, but I saw her headed to Leigh's room. I... don't know if she killed him. But when I saw Crystal in the hallway, headed to get blood for them, I got upset that I wasn't invited to play. So I went to talk to Ivonne. But she wasn't in the playroom." The words poured from her like machine-gun fire, the truth clear. "I don't know if she killed Leigh, but I know she wasn't in the playroom the whole time. And she'd been acting odd lately."

"Why didn't you tell anyone this before?" Aldric was texting Jayce as he spoke.

"Because she's a powerful member of the coven. And who would believe she'd killed her own mate? I was too afraid to ask. If she said no and I smelled her lie... she'd probably just kill me. She's terrifying."

"Then why do you sleep with her?"

The female blinked in surprise at the question. "She's rich and takes care of me. She takes care of all her staff."

Okay, then.

"That doesn't mean I'll sacrifice myself for her," Hilary continued, shaking her head.

"Where is she right now?"

The female shrugged. "How should I know?"

"That's not an answer."

She rolled her eyes, sat on the edge of the bed. "I really don't know. She said she had to run out. I think Crystal might have gone with her. She's not here either, that's all I know."

And clearly this female thought she'd take the opportunity to steal from Ivonne in the meantime.

As if she read his train of thought, she narrowed her eyes. "She won't notice any of this stuff missing. And she doesn't need it. She's rolling in money."

Jesus, whoever had created this female should be stabbed through the heart. She was the worst excuse for a vampire he'd ever met. And he'd met his share of narcissistic vamps.

"Don't leave this room. We've got the house locked down. If you try to run, you'll just piss me off." He let his wolf flare in his gaze for effect.

She flinched and nodded, not moving from her spot.

Still, he didn't think she'd stay put. Leaving the room, he texted the others, telling them to watch for anyone trying to jump from the second floor. Because instinct and past experience told him that was exactly what she would try to do.

Chapter 27

Natalia watched in fascination as sure enough, a female vampire opened a second-story window. The vamp looked around, paused, then climbed through it, a bag clutched in her hand, and jumped.

Wind whipped everywhere so Natalia had tucked her scarf tight around her neck. Scent and sounds didn't carry well with this kind of weather. If they hadn't been watching for the female, it would have been more difficult to track her.

"You two spread out to the other side of the house. I got this," Niko murmured, moving so fast he was nothing more than a blur.

Letting him take care of the female, Natalia nodded at Kat. They were patrolling the property while Jayce and Aldric were inside. So far nothing seemed out of the ordinary.

Using her supernatural speed, Natalia moved around the front of the house, looping back along the side until she was in the rear of the property.

Kat was right with her, stopping when she did. They both scanned the woods behind the house. Because of the recent snow, the only footprints Natalia could see were the ones they'd made in the last thirty minutes.

"So..." Kat shot her a sly look. "What's going on with you and Aldric?"

Natalia ignored her friend, continued scanning the woods. There was something in the air that bothered her, but she couldn't figure it out. "I don't think this is appropriate patrol talk."

Kat snorted. "Appropriate patrol talk? I might be new to the pack but even I know that's not a real thing."

"I... don't know." She glanced at Kat before looking away. "He's confusing." That being an understatement. She was still reeling from the way he'd been all possessive back at the B&B. It had been impossible not to ignore that he'd been staking a claim. But seriously, what the hell?

He wanted her, he wanted friendship, he wanted... what exactly? That was the problem. She had no idea. And she wasn't sure she was willing to take the risk of getting her heart shattered anyway.

"If it makes you feel any better, I think all males are confusing. At least shifter ones. They like to keep us on our toes."

It had taken Kat's mate forever to get his head out of his ass where she was concerned. Well, maybe not that long, but Kat liked to call her mate thick-headed.

"Heeell...." A strange animal sound carried on the sharp wind. It made all the hair on Natalia's neck stand on end.

"Did you hear that?" It was almost like a scream. When the wind whistled again she wasn't sure if it had just been the wind, nothing else.

Kat tilted her head to the side, then nodded. "Let's check it out."

It had come from the direction of the woods and might be nothing, might just be a wild animal. But they couldn't ignore it.

"I'm letting Jayce know," Kat added.

Natalia nodded. All bondmates had a telepathic link that let them communicate with each other.

As they moved toward the forest, a familiar lemony scent teased the air. "I scent the vampire employee, Crystal," Natalia murmured to Kat. "It could be an old scent trail." But with the weather, she doubted it.

Kat nodded in agreement. "Jayce just told me that they think Ivonne and Crystal left together."

Natalia and Kat picked up their pace as they entered the woods. There was more than enough moonlight illuminating the snow in front of them. There was also another scent in the air but Natalia couldn't figure out what it was. It tumbled away in the wind.

As a light snow started to fall, she continued to scan the woods while she and Kat jogged deeper into the forest.

"Jayce and Aldric aren't far behind us," Kat murmured.

Natalia nodded. It made her feel safer, knowing they had backup. Deeper and deeper into the woods they sprinted, following that lemony scent until...it disappeared.

They weren't in a clearing, exactly, but there was a slight opening among some trees, where the moonlight bathed the area. A few areas of snow had been disturbed. It was impossible to tell if the disturbance was from the weather, animals, or something else.

Looking up, Natalia cast her gaze over the trees, looking to see if the vampire, or vampires, were hiding in them.

That was something Aldric had taught her on one of their investigations. Something she'd never thought about before. He said that people always forgot to look up for threats. It was true. She was an apex predator and rarely thought about looking up for danger. It wasn't instinct to expect an attack from above.

Now, however, she slowly searched anywhere someone might hide. She moved to the shadows of the trees, using them as cover as she looked for any threat—

The ground gave way beneath her.

The air rushed from her lungs as she fell, but her inborn instinct refused to let her cry out even as panic punched through her. Her feet slammed into concrete at least ten feet below ground.

The impact jarred her. It took seconds to take in the scene before her: an underground dungeon with three cages. Each one held a prisoner. Two males who looked unconscious, and the female vampire, Crystal. Her cage door wasn't closed though. The female's eyes widened when she saw Natalia.

Natalia's claws extended as she prepared to jump back through the opening she'd fallen through. Crouching, she started to spring up when pain exploded in the back of her skull.

Stunned, but not knocked out, she swiveled to face her attacker, slashing out with her claws. She connected with clothing and flesh as a fist landed against her ribs.

She couldn't hear Kat, briefly wondered where her packmate was before raw survival instinct took over. Nothing else mattered except stopping this threat.

Her animal took over, her body shifting to wolf form without thought. The shift was almost instantaneous, much quicker than normal. Her bones shifted and realigned, her clothes shredding as fur replaced skin in seconds. It was so damn fast, there was no pain.

There was no room for emotions other than anger. She didn't care why she was being attacked, just that she was going to end this shit right now.

On all fours, she snarled at a bleeding, wild-eyed Ivonne. Looked as if Ivonne was guilty after all. Crouching low, she eyed the female, scanning for weapons and any sign of weakness as she prepared to attack.

Before she could move, a body slammed into her, throwing her against the wall. Crystal apparently wasn't a victim here. Natalia snarled. If she had to take on two attackers at once, so be it.

Chapter 28

Fear slid through Aldric's veins as he raced through the woods on all fours. After Kat had telepathed Jayce that she and Natalia were checking something out, he and Aldric had headed after them.

When not long after that, Kat told him she'd been caught in a trap and Natalia had fallen down a hole, his wolf had taken over. He could hear his brother racing behind him but didn't slow, didn't think of anything other than getting to Natalia.

He would not lose her. Not now. Not ever.

She was his. He'd failed one female and he couldn't fail this one. Losing Natalia... *No. Fuck, no.* It wasn't going to happen.

Even with the falling snow, her wild vanilla and cherry blossom scent rolled over him, calling to him like a beacon. As he breached a cluster of trees he instantly spotted Kat hanging from some sort of net.

"There!" she screamed, her claw-tipped finger pointing out through what had to be a silver-laced trap.

Snarling, Jayce raced toward his mate as Aldric sprinted to the barely visible opening. White drifts of snow partially covered a trapdoor. Pure instinct took over. Without thinking—or caring—about the consequences, he dove through the opening. He landed on all fours on the concrete floor with barely a sound.

Natalia had gone wolf, was ripping through the arm of a vampire female who was shrieking in pain. He couldn't see the female's face, didn't care who she was. If Natalia was attacking her, the female deserved it.

"Stupid fucking wolf!" Ivonne had a blade in her hand. Long and lean, she stalked toward Natalia, slashing up with the weapon as she lunged toward Natalia's back.

Aldric crouched low, using all the strength in his legs, and sprung at Ivonne.

She turned, blade in hand and made an inhuman snarl. Her eyes had gone a wild, bright amber as her own primal side took over.

He'd planned to go straight for her neck but when she raised the blade he shifted his momentum, rolling to the side at the last instant.

She struck out, the blade slicing along his ribs. The silver burned through his flesh and singed his fur. He barely noticed it.

Landing on all fours, he swiveled, facing off with her. Out of the corner of his eye he was aware of Natalia and the other female fighting. He wanted to go to her, to take out that vampire, but he kept his focus on Ivonne. He wouldn't do Natalia any good if he got killed.

The scent of Natalia's anger bled into the cavern, overriding his worry for her. She wasn't scared. She was pissed.

He had to have faith in her abilities. She was young but she was a strong wolf. And she trained often at the ranch.

Baring his canines, he circled Ivonne, who was holding her blade in one hand, extended claws tipping the other.

"You won't ruin this for me." Her voice shook, the sound almost animal as she slashed out at him.

He dodged back, avoiding another slice as she struck out. He didn't want to kill her, but he would if he had to. No, he wanted this bitch alive for her coven to deal with. For everyone to know that she'd been the one who'd tried to undermine the peace treaty—had killed her own fucking mate. There was no doubt in his mind she'd murdered Leigh, not when she had the two missing vampires in an underground dungeon. He couldn't imagine any reason good enough to murder your own mate so whatever her twisted logic was for trying to stop the peace treaty, no one would care.

He snapped his teeth at her, circling slowly around the small space. He watched her movements, evaluating her weaknesses.

He snapped his teeth again, which just seemed to enrage Ivonne. She dove at him, slashing with her claws this time. He ducked the blow, came up hard and sank his teeth into her elbow, ripping through the joint with a savage tear.

Just as quickly, he let go and slammed his heavier body into hers. She grunted and he felt the blade slice along his ribcage but he threw her off balance with a hard shove.

When Crystal screamed in agony, Ivonne screamed as well. Aldric wanted to turn around, to make sure Natalia was okay, but Ivonne was the bigger threat. He had to incapacitate her, or if it came down to saving Natalia's life, kill Ivonne. Nothing could stop him from saving the woman he loved.

Blood poured down Ivonne's limp arm, pooling on the concrete below. Threads of tendons were the only thing keeping the limb attached. The metallic scent of her blood filled the air. "Stupid fucking wolves, trying to take everything from me!" She threw her head back and let out a shriek before lunging for him.

He rose up on his back paws, giving her a perfect target. At the last minute, using supernatural speed and her own momentum against her, he ducked low, ramming into her legs.

Bone cracked as he made impact with her knees. Her scream ripped through the air as she thudded against the concrete.

Moving lightning fast, he pinned her to the floor, a heavy paw on her remaining arm as he wrapped his jaws around her throat. He pressed down, drawing blood, but didn't tear through her neck like his wolf wanted him to.

His most primal side simply wanted to end this female's life, to completely eliminate the threat to Natalia. He cared nothing for politics or the job he'd been hired to do.

All that mattered was Natalia's safety.

The battle waged in his mind for only seconds before he let his human half take control. At the same moment, Jayce dropped down into the prison.

With gloved hands he stalked toward them carrying what looked like silver ropes of some sort.

Aldric moved off Ivonne, but not before raking his teeth against her neck in an act of pure aggression. She howled her agony, but he knew it wouldn't kill her. Iron-tinged blood filled his mouth. He spit it out as his brother rolled the whimpering vampire to her stomach and hogtied her with the silver ropes.

Trusting his brother to have his back, he whirled to face Natalia, who'd shifted back to human form. Patches of blood covered her naked body and Crystal's decapitated corpse lay a few feet away.

Growling, he shifted, the change slower this time now that adrenaline wasn't punching through him. As the pain passed, he'd barely pushed to his feet when Natalia's arms wrapped around him. The skin-to-skin contact soothed him even as his primal side reacted to the feel of her naked body against his. He was close to carrying her out of there, to hell with everything else.

"You're okay?" he asked, holding her tight. He wanted to run his hands over her, to check for injuries, but she was gripping him too firmly.

And he didn't want to let her go.

"Yes," she rasped out. "I didn't want to kill her, but she left me no choice." A sob ripped from her throat, her petite body trembling.

Fuck. Fuck this whole situation. He hated that she'd been put in a position to kill again. She might be tough and full of attitude, but killing another being wasn't something that would come easy to her.

Her heart was too soft, too sweet.

He cradled the back of her head, angled his own body in front of her so she couldn't see the corpse. He stroked down her back, tracing his hand up and down her spine, ignoring Ivonne's cries of pain. They needed to free Darius and Arthur, who looked worse for wear as they came out of their unconsciousness, and get Ivonne back to her coven leader to face justice for what she'd done.

But for just a moment longer, he was going to hold on to the female he loved. The female he never wanted to let go.

And be grateful that she was alive, that he'd gotten here in time. Without saying a word, he moved underneath the entrance, and, using all the strength in his body, propelled them out of that hellhole. He'd go back down there, but he wanted her away from the blood and death.

Chapter 29

Natalia sat next to Kat on a bright purple velvet settee while Jayce and Aldric stood guard in front of them. After taking Ivonne to her coven leader, and freeing the Clifton vampires—and finding some clothing for Natalia, Kat and Aldric, since theirs had all been shredded during their shifts—they were all in a huge room in Elian Clifton's mansion.

Kat had been burned by the silver of the trap in the woods but she was mostly healed—and had made it clear to Jayce and anyone with ears that she wasn't missing this meeting.

Aldric and Jayce stood in front of her and Kat, basically guarding them. She understood that their wolves were feeling irrationally overprotective right now. It didn't matter that the threat was neutralized. They hadn't had any time alone since bringing Ivonne to Elian to be dealt with. Aldric had been incredibly gentle with her. Being near him made Natalia feel safe, even if she didn't trust that feeling. Too many emotions bombarded her and she needed distance from him.

"She needs to be publicly executed," Constance demanded. She was sitting on Darius's lap. She'd tried to stand a couple times, but the newly-freed male wasn't letting her go.

Elian Clifton, polished as ever, had his arms crossed over his chest as he stood next to Craig Kinley. The vampire coven leader and the shifter Alpha looked like a united front. Which boded well for the peace treaty.

Craig cleared his throat and looked pointedly at Aldric. "You are welcome to stay for this, as the Brethren hired you."

There was a long pause and it took Natalia a moment to realize he meant that the rest of them—her, Kat, Jayce and Niko—needed to leave.

It made sense, and she was so freaking tired she couldn't even be offended. Because the truth was, they'd been hired to do a job. They'd done it. She didn't care how Ivonne was punished. As long as she was. Wasn't her business what happened from here.

She stood at the same time Kat did. Aldric moved soundlessly, sliding an arm around Natalia's waist, holding her close. "I'll come with you."

She shook her head. "No, finish this. It's important." And it was. He needed to be here to accurately document what happened for the Brethren, and probably to question Ivonne himself. Then this job would be over.

Aldric's body vibrated with tension so she pressed a hand to his chest. She didn't care about the others in the room, didn't care about anything except him right now. She still wasn't sure what would happen between them and it wasn't something she could focus on at the moment.

Nodding tightly, he said, "I'll be back as soon as I can."

As she stepped away from Aldric, Jayce moved up to her, wrapped his free arm around her shoulders to guide both her and Kat from the room. They didn't need the escort, but the tension completely ebbed from Aldric's face as he watched them go.

Because he trusted his brother to watch out for her.

When they were finally outside the mansion, Natalia nudged Jayce. "Dude, I'm fine." Physically, at least. She hadn't been cut with any silver, just a few superficial claw wounds that had already healed. She'd killed that vampire in self-defense, but that didn't mean she had to be okay with taking another life. Trembles wanted to overtake her, but she managed to keep her reaction hidden. Aldric had tried to comfort her as much as he could but she'd had to keep it together so they could free the males and get Ivonne—and Crystal's body—back here.

"I swear to God if either you say you're fine one more time…" Jayce's grip around her tightened once but then he let her go. He didn't let go of Kat, however.

Kat rolled her eyes. "We *are* fine. It was just some surface burns. I'm fine now. Fine, fine, fine." She shoved up the sleeve of the borrowed T-shirt someone had given her to show completely unmarred skin.

"Maybe you should see a healer," Natalia said.

Kat looked at her as if she was a traitor. "You can't take his side."

"I'm not. I just… silver poisoning is scary." She'd lost her parents and so many pack members to it a year ago. Way too many. Kat seemed completely fine but the paranoid part of Natalia's brain wanted her friend to get checked out. Just to be cautious. Her throat tightened at the thought of something happening to Kat simply because she hadn't gone to a healer.

"Hell, I wasn't even thinking about… I'm sorry, Natalia." Distress rolled off her in waves. Kat frowned, looked at Jayce. "For the record, I don't think I need one, but I'll see a healer."

"I'll make sure Natalia gets back to the B&B safely," Niko said to Jayce.

"*She* is standing right here."

Giving her a half-smile, he shrugged. "Come on, I need to get back before sunrise anyway."

"Oh, right." She turned to Kat. "Text me when you get to the healer, let me know what she says?" The Kinley pack had a very rare healer—Natalia's own pack didn't have one—who'd already offered her assistance to all of them.

"I will."

Once in the SUV with Niko behind the wheel, Natalia leaned back against the passenger seat. She wanted a shower and her own clean clothes.

"What do you think will happen to Ivonne?" she asked as he steered down the street. They were still in Clifton territory.

"Once they finish questioning her, figure out the depth of her betrayal, she'll definitely be executed. If it's up to the coven, they'll drag her torture out for years. Decades, maybe."

She straightened in her seat. She'd known that vampires didn't balk at torture, but that seemed excessive, even for them. "What?"

"Killing her outright is nothing. It doesn't send a strong enough message to vampires. And my kind…" He paused, took a left turn out of the gated community. "They need to know that undermining their coven leader will never, ever be tolerated. Simple death isn't a deterrence, but the thought of decades of some of the most brutal torture will make someone think twice before betraying their leader or coven."

"Shifters really are different," she murmured.

He gave her a simple nod and they continued on in silence. When they reached the B&B she found a huge breakfast had been prepared for them by the proprietor. Though she hadn't thought she'd be able to eat anything, the scent of bacon and pancakes proved her wrong.

An hour later she'd eaten, showered and, even though she was exhausted, was anxiously awaiting word from Aldric and Kat. Kat finally texted, saying she was fine and that Natalia and Jayce were like old ladies worrying about her.

When Aldric texted her, her heart rate kicked up about a hundred notches just seeing his name on her screen. *Peace treaty still moving forward. Have to interrogate Ivonne then wrap up a few more things but I'll be back in a couple hours. Then we're going to finish what we started.*

A rush of heat blistered through her. Seeing the unexpected words took her off guard. Setting her phone in her lap, she stared at it for a long moment, emotions spiraling through her in an out-of-control tidal wave.

Now that the case was over there was nothing in the way of...what? She'd forgiven him for the way he'd cut and run all those months ago. Knowing what she did about his past, what he'd been through, how could she not? But that didn't mean she was ready to jump into a relationship.

She was a mess right now, her emotions too conflicted. If she was here when Aldric got back, she knew she'd fall into bed with him. Before—or if—that ever happened, she needed distance. Needed to get her head on straight. And the truth was, she needed to know that he was damn sure *she* was who he wanted.

Emotions had been high during this investigation and the only reason things had originally sparked between them was because Aldric had gotten jealous of seeing Niko with her.

If that hadn't happened, she wasn't even sure if, after the case was finished, he'd have come back to the ranch. Come back to *her*.

And she needed to know that he would come for her. That she was a female worth pursuing. The not knowing would eat at her forever. She didn't want to play games with him, and this wasn't a game. But she had to know he'd come for her.

Once she was packed she wrote a note, left it on his bed so he'd be sure to see it, then headed home. The last two sentences of her note made things crystal clear. *It's all or nothing with me. Make sure you know what you want.* Now it was up to him.

Chapter 30

Aldric resisted the urge to leave Elian's home, to go straight to Natalia. He had to finish this job. Once it was done, nothing was keeping him from her.

It bothered him that she hadn't returned his text, but she was dealing with a lot, had just killed someone. And he wanted to be there for her.

He turned his phone to silent as he followed Elian to the holding cell below his mansion. The coven leader was allowing Aldric to talk to Ivonne first since he was working for the Brethren, but mainly since he'd been the one to capture her.

It was the only reason this male would allow him to speak to the female. The rage rolling off Elian was contained, but barely.

Elian punched in a code on the security panel when they reached the dungeon door. "We'll be watching," he murmured before pushing the door open.

Aldric stepped inside, eyeing the captive female. Still in her ripped, blood-stained clothing, Ivonne's wrists and ankles were restrained by silver manacles. The scent of her burning flesh was offensive to his senses, but he didn't let it show as he shut the door behind him. He didn't bother looking at the two-way mirror as he sat in the chair across from her.

"You can talk to me or your coven leader." He wouldn't waste time with lies or cajoling her. "You know he'll torture you and nothing I say will change that. Nothing I *do* will change that. You've betrayed your people."

"They betrayed *me*," she spat, her amber eyes brightening, that hint of madness he'd seen before clear now.

"If you didn't want to be part of the treaty, you could have left your coven." Nothing held her to her people. She wasn't indentured to Elian, and a free vampire could move anywhere she chose. She had no excuse for what she'd done.

Aldric didn't think this was about the treaty, however. Not really.

She didn't respond to his statement and he didn't expect her to. He wasn't certain how hard she would be to break and he didn't relish the idea of torturing anyone. The truth was, he'd leave that to Elian. He didn't want any more blood on his hands.

"If you answer my questions, you'll receive your sentencing instead of being tortured by Elian." A technical truth. She might be tortured after what would definitely be a death sentence, and likely by someone not Elian. No scent of a lie rolled off him.

It was clear she understood his word games, however, when her lips curved into a sneer. "My sentencing will be torture before death. They'll keep me alive for decades before they kill me."

Something told him she'd try to kill herself long before then. And that she might be successful. He could never do what the vampires did—stretch out punishments so long—but he understood why that kind of punishment needed to happen in the vampire world. "You're probably right. But if you don't answer my questions, everyone who has ever worked for you will die. Including their families, if they have them." He let his words sink in, let the truth roll off him.

He hated that it was true, that Elian would mete out a swift, brutal punishment on the chance that anyone who worked for her knew of her treachery. Vampires were such a brutal species, even more brutal than shifters. Families were off-limits to his kind, but vamps...they needed the fear inside them that if they betrayed their leaders, there was only a scorched earth policy in place.

Aldric wasn't certain he'd allow Elian to go that far, however. He didn't think his brother would either. They'd intervene before that happened. But Ivonne didn't know that. So he tried to play on whatever shred of conscience she might have.

"You want all those deaths on your conscience? Think long and hard about all the pain and suffering you'll cause. Is that your final legacy?"

She didn't respond, just watched him with an ice-cold gaze.

He gave it one more shot. "On the off chance there is an afterlife for you, do you think you'll ever get to meet up with your first mate with all those deaths on your head?"

Ivonne stared hard at him for a long moment, clenched and unclenched her jaw. "Ask your questions," she rasped out.

"You killed Leigh, your mate."

She nodded once.

"Answer audibly."

"Yes, I killed Leigh. I never considered him my true mate though. My mate was killed by Craig Kinley," she snarled, yanking against her chains.

And there it was. The reason behind everything. Her admission only confirmed what he'd thought.

The chains rattled as she strained but she would never get out of them. She had to be in incredible pain now but her rage seemed to be fueling her struggle against the bonds.

"So Craig killed your mate? No one ever knew?" Because not even Elian had known who'd killed him. Ivonne's mate had been a casualty of one of the pack-coven battles hundreds of years ago.

Rage morphed to raw anguish on her face, she nodded. "Yes. I saw him murder my beloved Paulos. I held him in my arms for days." Blood-tinged tears tracked down her face.

Aldric felt the smallest amount of pity for the female, but didn't allow it to show in his body language or scent.

"That animal cut him down like a rag doll. Shredded his beautiful body. I...wanted to kill Kinley, would have if I hadn't been wounded so badly."

"Why wait hundreds of years to go after him?"

She made a scoffing sound. "He's impossible to get to, too strong for me. I'm not stupid enough to think I could best him physically. And I didn't want to kill him. Not right away anyway. I wanted him to suffer the way I did, to feel agony for centuries." Her amber eyes brightened. "I was so fucking close."

"So what was the plan? Kill your mate and blame Constance? Why kidnap the others?"

"Leigh was the only one who would have died… potentially. I planned to eventually let Arthur and Darius free. After Constance had been executed for killing Leigh and enough evidence pointed to her doing the same to Arthur and Darius, I would have freed them."

Her scent was muddied, as if she wasn't sure what she'd have truly done with the other two males.

"How did you keep them in those cages?" Once the doors were unlocked and opened they'd been able to walk out. But when the doors in that dungeon were closed, it was impossible for them to escape. Aldric figured it was a witch but he wanted to get every answer he could.

"I ambushed both of them, which you must know. As for the cages, a witch spelled them for me." She absently swiped at some of the drying tears.

"Where's the witch now?"

Ivonne lifted an eyebrow. "Where do you think?"

He didn't respond, just watched her.

The vampire let out a huff of annoyance. "She's dead."

"How did you get Arthur to meet you?" Arthur had been certain he'd spoken on the phone to a male named Hamish, Kinley's second-in-command.

She lifted a shoulder, the chains rattling again. "Human technology."

"You recorded his voice?"

"It's more complicated than that, but yes. And it took a very, very long time to get all the words and right inflections from Hamish recorded. Luckily time wasn't an issue for me."

Aldric was familiar with the type of software she referred to and planned to have all her electronics ripped apart to see if she'd recorded anyone else's voice. "How'd you get Constance's scent all over the murder scene?"

"When I kidnapped Darius, I took a bunch of Constance's belongings from his house. The place stank of her." Ivonne's lips curved up in disgust. "All I had to do was leave her belongings on my bed and rub them against Leigh. His blood held the scent well."

"Did you do anything else to try to frame Constance?" He knew the answer, but needed it on record.

"I took some of Arthur's blood when he was unconscious, splattered it around the back of Constance's SUV." She said it so calmly.

Jesus, maybe he didn't feel sorry for her. This female was pathological. To be able to do that to her own mate and a coven member was beyond horrific. "I want all the names of everyone who knew of your treachery."

Turned out it was just Crystal, but he still went through every person who had ever worked for her or been to her house, and asked her specific questions to gauge if she was lying. Hours later, he was done. Elian would interrogate her himself, would have to personally talk to everyone in his coven, but that wasn't Aldric's concern. He had all the information he needed to officially close this case and get back to Natalia.

He met Elian, Darius, Constance, Kinley, Arthur and Ursula in a sitting room on one of the upper levels. Most of them had witnessed his questioning via cameras in the room, but he was certain Elian and Kinley had watched from behind the two-way mirror. Their scents had been strong in the air.

"The Brethren will want a full report from you regarding what you find out from the rest of your coven," Aldric said, not bothering to make small talk. He wanted to be gone hours ago, wanted to get to Natalia.

Elian nodded. "They will have it." His voice was blade sharp.

"What's her sentencing?" It would be death, that much was certain, but he wanted to know what would happen to the female before then.

Elian looked at Constance and her father. "I believe you two deserve the right to decide."

To Aldric's surprise, the Alpha looked at his daughter. "She kidnapped your mate, wanted to frame you for murder and have you executed. The decision is yours."

Constance held Darius's hand in hers, squeezed tight. "A quick, merciful death." She didn't pause in her declaration.

The room fell silent and for the first time in ages, Aldric found himself truly surprised.

The shifter princess lifted a shoulder. "She's a psycho bitch, but... maybe she'll be reunited with her first mate in the afterlife. To have that much rage and hate inside her for centuries... I think she's suffered enough. And I don't want to be responsible for someone else's suffering. Not like that."

Darius pulled the tall female into his arms, brushed his lips over her cheek. "You're too merciful."

"Maybe, but this treaty needs to go forward and I don't want to think of her ever again."

Aldric moved back toward the door, opened it as the others began talking amongst themselves. These were pack-coven issues that had no bearing on him. He'd done what he'd come to do.

Now it was time to find and claim the female he loved.

Chapter 31

Three days later

Tension sharp in her shoulders, Natalia did her best to ignore it as she trekked from her Alpha's house to hers. Her sister Gloria was in town working for a few hours, which meant she'd have the house all to herself. Sometimes that was a really good thing, and sometimes it wasn't. Her wolf needed solitude on occasion, but right now she didn't want to be alone.

Three fucking days and she hadn't heard a word from Aldric. She'd really thought—

She froze at the sight of him sitting on her front steps. His long, muscular, jean-clad legs were stretched out in front of him and a long-sleeved T-shirt molded to all of his very delectable muscles. A duffel bag was behind him near the front door. His dark scent, the one that reminded her of a place deep in the woods that had never been touched by humans, teased her, caressed her senses.

Annoyance and hunger for him battled inside her. Whenever she was near him she had to steel herself against the way he made her feel. She'd never experienced anything like it before.

He immediately stood as she approached, watching her carefully as if he was afraid she might bolt.

"When did you get in town?" she demanded.

"Two and a half days ago."

She blinked and a knife slid right between her ribs. If he'd been here all this time then why the hell hadn't he come to see her? She reached the bottom step, stood a couple feet from him. She shoved her hands in her pockets. "Kat said everything went well with the wrap-up of the investigation." She wasn't sure how she kept her voice civil. She didn't want to talk about the fucking investigation. She wanted to ream him out.

"It did. I don't want to talk about that though." The deep cadence of his voice was another caress over her senses as his eyes went wolf.

Her heart rate increased being this close to him. Even thinking about him got her worked up, but being around him in person had all her senses on edge. She wanted to reach out and stroke him, touch him. And okay, she wanted to punch him a little bit too. It was a love-hate thing battling inside her. "Okay. Let's talk." Her voice was icy.

Heat flared in his gaze, his hunger unmistakable. And if she'd somehow missed that, his scent intensified, letting her know how much he was affected by her.

Her own body reacted in turn, her nipples hardening against her bra. Her wolf was going crazy, clawing her up, excited that he was finally here. *Stupid biology.* She cleared her throat.

"Can we go inside?" he half-growled.

Oh, she wanted to, but she didn't trust herself. And she needed to know what he had to say first. There was no longer an investigation looming over them, no threat. It was just the two of them. "We can sit on the porch." She strode up the few steps, conscious of his gaze on her and the way nerves danced in her belly at the thought of him watching, wanting. The swing creaked as she perched on the edge of it.

"Thank you for the note." Every line in his body tense, he didn't sit next to her, but leaned against the front porch railing, watching her.

"I can't tell if you're being sarcastic."

He shoved out a breath. "I'm not."

She hadn't wanted to leave without telling him where she'd gone. It would have been wrong. Still, she couldn't do just a sexual relationship or even a regular mating. She wanted everything. When she mated, it was going to be for life. "Before we were interrupted that last night, you said you'd been fighting your feelings for me since we met."

He nodded and she realized his claws had extended, were digging into the railing of the porch as he watched her. "I had been. I'm not anymore. I know I don't deserve a chance with you, but I'm asking for one. I want your friendship, but I want a whole lot fucking more than just that. I can never be simply your friend. It's impossible."

"What *do* you want?" Because yeah, she wanted—needed—it spelled out.

His expression softened, melting her a teeny bit. "To give you everything you could ever want, to protect you, to love you." His voice trembled slightly as he spoke, the action out of character for the huge male.

Her heart squeezed. He was offering her everything she'd ever wanted from him. But she was afraid to really believe him. She pushed up from the swing. "How do I know you won't freak out again and leave? How do I know I won't come in second to your dead mate?" That was her real fear, the one she couldn't seem to shake.

"The first one, you won't know. I can tell you I won't, but showing you is the only thing I can do. And I'm not going anywhere." He stepped forward, crowding her personal space until she had to step back to the wall. "I'm not letting you go, Natalia. You're mine."

She flicked a glance to the duffel bag, wondered about it, but didn't comment before turning to him again. Her heart was racing out of control, a staccato beat in her chest she wished she could get under control.

Reaching out, he cupped her jaw, the action impossibly tender. "As for coming in second? You could never come in second. To anything or anyone."

She wanted to lean into his touch, to rub up against him. But... "I'm not sweet and submissive!" The words were out before she could think about reining them in. And screw it—she didn't want to hold anything back. Not with him and not about this. It was too important. She was terrified that she'd never live up to the female he'd been mated to. That later, once the lust burned out, he'd look at her and only feel regret.

He blinked and she realized she'd surprised him. His hand slid around to cup the back of her head. "I'm... well aware that you're not submissive. It's one of the reasons I fell so hard for you."

Her shoulders eased. "Really?"

His scent made her crazy. "I like your attitude and occasionally dirty mouth." His gaze flicked to her lips, then moved back to her eyes, all hunger and need there. "I like that you say what's on your mind. You don't put up with shit from anyone, me included. But you're wrong about one thing. You might not be submissive, but you have a very sweet, big heart."

Part of her wanted to shove him back, to keep a barrier between them. He was wreaking havoc on her heart and she wasn't sure she could handle it. This male had the capability to destroy her and she was so afraid he would let her down again. But she didn't want to be a coward, to run from something that could be amazing simply to protect herself. Because in the end, she'd lose him either way. "Why'd you wait to come see me?" She'd been in agony the last three days.

"I... chased you here immediately, was ready to hunt you down. I didn't trust myself around you. Didn't trust my wolf not to simply take you away from here, to claim you in every single way without talking about it first. I wanted to fuck you until neither of us could walk, until I bound you to me with pure pleasure."

Heat surged through her as everything feminine inside her flared to life. He grasped one of her hands with his free one. She loved the feel of his callused fingers against hers.

"I love you, Natalia," he growled, his fingers tightening on the back of her head. "Have for a long time. What I feel for you eclipses anything I've felt for anyone. Ever."

His words enveloped her, both female and wolf accepting the raw truth. She wasn't coming in second, never would. Her heart cracked open as she accepted that she loved him too. Had for far too long. She'd been in lust with him ever since he'd saved her from those vampires hell-bent on killing her, when he hadn't even known who she was. The love hadn't been far behind that.

God, that seemed like a lifetime ago. Unexpected tears stung her eyes. Blinking them away, she started to tell him that she loved him too, but he put a finger over her lips.

"Don't respond. I haven't earned your trust yet, but I will."

She nipped his finger lightly and he growled low in his throat. They might have to forge trust with each other still, but he was here, laying himself bare to her.

She wouldn't be a coward, not when he was everything she'd ever wanted. If she walked away from him, from what they might have, she was a fool. Her wolf wouldn't let her anyway. She was way too possessive of this male. The thought of letting him go, of someone else touching him... Nope.

"I have the house all to myself." The softly spoken words weren't at all what she'd been about to say, but now that she'd said them, she didn't want to take them back. Heat flooded between her thighs as his grayish-green eyes darkened with hunger.

Without giving him a chance to respond, she moved lightning fast, ducking away from him and into the house. She'd barely taken two steps inside before he was on her, slamming the door behind them.

She loved being chased, knew it was a wolf thing. It didn't matter that she wasn't submissive outside the bedroom, she still craved for him to take complete control in bed.

His mouth crushed over hers as one hand slid to the back of her skull, holding her tight. A shudder racked her body as she moaned into his mouth. Kissing him felt like coming home.

She leaned into him, linking her fingers behind his neck as she tried to climb him. They'd both seen each other in stages of nudity, and she'd most definitely been able to appreciate what he looked like after a shift. Back in the underground prison she'd been too traumatized to appreciate him. And normally she tried to avoid staring too hard and getting caught.

Now she didn't have to pretend she wasn't turned on, didn't have to avoid looking. And she wanted to see every single inch of him right now. She reached for the button of his jeans but he grasped her wrists, growling softly against her mouth as he tugged them away.

He pulled back, his eyes bright with need. "I get to taste you first."

It took all of a second for her to realize what he meant. Another shot of heat flooded between her thighs. She cleared her throat. "I've never... had anyone do that." And she really, really wanted Aldric to, even if she was nervous.

"You're really are a virgin." He rasped the words out, not exactly a question.

"Yes."

He growled again, this one harsher than before, as he lifted her into his arms.

She let out a little yelp, but twisted slightly so that she could wrap her legs around his waist. She couldn't get close enough to him. Wanting to tease him, to make him crazy, she nibbled little kisses along his jaw as he walked them to... somewhere.

He sucked in a sharp breath when she not-so-lightly bit his earlobe, the energy rolling off him intense as his grip on her ass tightened.

She couldn't seem to focus on anything, including their surroundings. When he laid her down in front of the living room fireplace, covering her body with his, she arched into him.

"Naked, now," she demanded. She wanted to stroke her fingertips over every single inch of his muscular, delectable body. She was tired of not being able to touch the only male she'd ever craved. It was as if she'd come alive with sensuality when they'd met, then she hadn't been able to do a damn thing about it.

His mouth curved up in the sexiest, most wicked grin as he crouched in front of her. Ignoring her demand, he kept his gaze pinned to hers as he slowly unbuttoned her jeans. Instead of tugging them off, he simply pulled the zipper down, but nothing else.

Her breasts were heavy with need, her nipples tightened into painful beads as her inner walls clenched, desperate to be filled by him. She might not have any experience with males, but she knew exactly what she needed right now. Aldric inside her.

She reached for him, ready to strip all of his clothes off, but he moved back onto the balls of his feet, crouching in between her spread legs.

"I'm getting my fill of you first." His voice was deep, seductive.

Breathing erratically, she shook her head. "I want to see all of you." Her words came out a shaky plea.

"Soon." The gleam in his eyes told her she wouldn't regret doing as he ordered. Still, she wanted to strip him bare. Before she could respond he reached for the hem of her sweater, tugged it over her head.

When Natalia was completely bared to him, all the air left Aldric's lungs. He'd seen her naked in different situations, but seeing her full breasts all ripe and his to taste, to tease, his cock shoved at his jeans.

This female had the ability to destroy him. He couldn't imagine another day without her in his life. When he hadn't been looking, she'd *become* his life.

He wasn't letting her go.

Knowing she hadn't been touched by another male did something to his most primitive side. He wouldn't have cared if she hadn't been a virgin, but knowing he was going to be her first—and her last—made him feel a hundred fucking feet tall.

And terrified he'd fuck this up.

Bring her as much pleasure as she could take—that was his number one goal. Realizing he was staring, he moved into action.

Her slender fingers slid up his chest, clutched onto his shoulders as he dipped a head to her breast.

Her fingers dug into him, just the tips of claws pricking his skin as he barely bit down on her light brown nipple.

"Aldric." His name came out as a moan as she arched her back, trying to push deeper into his mouth.

He pulled back, blew on the glossy, hard bud. God, he wanted to devour this female.

She shuddered, the scent of her lust as sweet as her natural cherry blossom scent. She invaded his veins, made him crazy with a hunger that he had to shove back. Right now was all about her, about making her scream his name as she came against his tongue.

His cock jerked again, his erection hard and painful. Too fucking bad.

She rolled her hips against him as he slowly teased her other breast.

"You know...how many times I fantasized about this," she whispered, the words not quite a question.

He growled low in his throat. He could imagine because he'd probably had the same fucking fantasies. His were probably dirtier though.

Her claws pricked his shoulders again when he nipped at the sensitive underside of a breast.

The pleasure-pain sent a punch of sensation through him, making his cock pulse. He loved that she didn't apologize for the use of claws, as if she knew he craved everything she had to give.

"I need more!" she cried out.

He laughed against her breast even as he continued lower, his hands gliding along her ribs and waist. "So demanding."

She simply rolled her hips, her breathing growing more erratic as he kissed lower, lower... He kissed all along her abdomen, teasing the sensitive skin right above her unbuttoned jeans.

Her scent was pure heaven, growing stronger by the second. He wanted to plunge deep into her with his cock, to claim her, but it was too soon for that.

Even if she disagreed with him, he wasn't fully taking her tonight. But he was going to taste her, hear what she sounded like when she came.

The wire tethering his control grew taut, almost snapped, as he tugged her jeans and thong down her lean legs. He tossed her clothes to the side and stared down at the juncture between her legs. With a shaking hand, he barely teased a finger down her silky, pink folds.

She made a soft sigh of pleasure, barely rolling her hips.

Inhaling, he drew in her scent, every part of him feeling primal with the demand to take her. He held back though, taking his time. If this was her first time experiencing this, he was going to make damn sure she came. More than once by the time the night was over.

When he traced his finger down her folds again, she shuddered and moaned. "Aldric," she whispered. The sound was pure music to his soul, soothing all of him.

Natalia, the female he'd been fantasizing about forever, was right here, moaning out his name.

Reaching up her body, he cupped a breast, tweaked a hard nipple as he buried his face between her legs. He wanted to inundate her with sensation. He'd been serious when he'd told her he hadn't trusted himself not to hunt her down and claim her. He felt the need now, driving him hard.

He'd wanted to go slower, to work her up even more, but he couldn't not taste what was right in front of him.

"Oh..." She let out a garbled moan as his tongue flicked up her soaked folds.

She was so fucking wet. All for him.

Mine.

His wolf knew that without a doubt, the mating instinct a live thing inside him, demanding he take her from behind under the full moon, mark her with his teeth so everyone knew she was his. Off-limits.

He shoved that primitive side back down, focused on her clit.

Her fingers thrust through his hair, holding onto his head as he ate at her, so fucking hungry for her he could come right then and there. He should be embarrassed by that, but this female pulled him inside out. He wanted to bring her so much pleasure that she had no doubt who she belonged to.

Him.

He slid a finger inside her, moaned against her folds as he felt just how tight she was. Her inner walls clenched around him, drawing him in.

He added another.

"Aldric," she rasped out, his name a prayer on her perfect lips.

He increased pressure on her clit, didn't let up as she rolled her hips over and over, meeting him stroke for stroke. She'd probably had an orgasm before from her own touch but he hoped he was the first to do this for her.

He knew when she was close, could feel the way her sheath grew tighter, slicker. When she surged into orgasm, he still didn't let up. He kept teasing her clit with each ragged cry that tore from her throat.

Until she grew limp, her fingers just stroking against his hair. "Holy..." She practically purred. "That was incredible." Her voice was soft, sensual.

Breathing hard, he looked up the length of her body, drinking in every inch of her bare skin until he met her gaze. "You're incredible."

Smiling, she pushed up, stretched out her hands for him.

He grasped them, slid his fingers through hers. "Not...tonight." He barely forced the words out, hoping she understood. He couldn't lose control tonight. She didn't deserve that her first time, and when they finally crossed that line he wanted to bond with her. Not just mate.

"Fuck that," she snarled, ripping at the button of his jeans, shoving them down to his hips.

He told himself to stop her, but simply couldn't, not when she looked so fierce, so beautiful. She wrapped her fist around his cock, pumped him once, twice, harder, harder, her grip intense.

The sensation was pure. Fucking. Heaven. His fantasies didn't come close to what the actual feel of her touching him was like. "I want your come on me. I want your scent all over me." She was still practically snarling at him, her dark eyes seeming brighter.

Fuck him.

He stared into her dark, blazing eyes, this brave female who'd completely stolen his heart, before slanting his mouth over hers.

She moaned into him, would have to taste herself on him. He wondered if she liked the way she tasted and *that* thought made his entire body jolt. It took all his control not to flip her onto her knees, to slide into her from behind and lose himself.

She continued pumping him, as if she already understood his body and what he wanted. Growling into her mouth, he savored the feel of her hand wrapped around him, her soft palm against his cock. He'd fantasized about this countless times, but having her actually touching him, stroking him, was better than any fantasy.

Finally he let go of his control, coming on her hand and stomach in long, hot jets. He tore his mouth from hers and gasped for breath, watching her face as he found his release.

Keeping his gaze pinned to hers, he reached between their bodies, rubbed his essence into her. He didn't care how primal it was. He wanted his scent on her as much as she wanted it. Hell, he wanted it embedded in her, so deep that no one could mistake who she belonged to.

"I love you too, by the way."

Her voice was clear. She wasn't saying the words through a fog of lust. All the muscles in his body pulled tight at her admission. It was more than he'd dared hope for right now. Especially after the way he'd broken her trust.

But he was a selfish bastard and he would take her love. Take it and give everything back to her.

Leaning down, he brushed his lips over hers but pulled back at the sound of the front door opening. "Nat, why is there a bag on the front porch—"

Natalia pushed at his chest, her eyes wide. "Don't come in!" she shouted before burying her face in his chest.

There was a long pause, then. "Oh my God! It smells like a freaking brothel in here. You two better clean up!" Gloria's muted giggles trailed off as the door slammed shut.

Aldric laughed as Natalia just pulled him down onto her, wrapping her arms around him. She kissed his mouth as if she was starving for him, as if they hadn't just brought each other to release.

He kissed her back with the same intensity because the truth was, he was starving for her too. He would never get enough of her either.

This female owned him, body and soul.

Chapter 32

One month later

Natalia forced herself not to run as she made her way to Teresa, Ryan and Lucas's place. Tonight was *the* night. And she wanted to talk to her big sister. Because, okay, she was a little freaked out at the thought of bonding.

Aldric had been stupidly insistent that they wait until now to have sex. Like he was still punishing himself over the way he'd run from her. Or she assumed that was the reason why. He'd been frustratingly vague on the reason.

Well, now he was just punishing her. The fooling around was fun—beyond fun—but she wanted everything from him. And he was going to give it to her.

Tonight.

She wanted to talk to Teresa because she was just curious about the other stuff that went with bonding. Like the telepathic link. Bonded couples had that ability but no one really talked about it much.

When she reached the front porch, she let out a little laugh at the sight of Vivian and Lucas passed out sleeping near the front door. Lucas was a ten-, or maybe eleven-year-old by now, wolf pup that Ryan had adopted. Vivian, a rambunctious jaguar cub who'd been adopted by their Alpha couple—and pretty much everyone else in the pack—was curled up fast asleep in her jaguar form, with Lucas wrapped around her protectively in his lupine form.

The little boy was huge for a pup his age and Natalia had a feeling he'd one day be an Alpha. The way he acted around Vivian, even for one so young, was with the sort of protective actions of a full-grown wolf.

A plate with only crumbs on it sat a foot away from them. She smiled at the sight of them. It had been a long time since they'd had young on the ranch and she loved the life they brought to it.

As if sensing her presence, Vivian opened her big, bright green eyes and made a soft purring sound at Natalia. Yeah, there was no way she could resist picking the little munchkin up. But when she stepped forward to scoop her up, Lucas wrapped a paw around Vivian's middle without opening his eyes.

Vivian made a purring sound and instead of jumping for Natalia, curled back into Lucas's embrace.

"He informed me that he'd be mating with her one day." Ryan's amused voice made Natalia smile.

She turned to find her brother-in-law leaning against the now open front door. She'd heard it open but hadn't wanted to tear her gaze away from these two. There was just something about the sweetness of the little ones. It made all the bad shit in the world fade away, at least for a few uninterrupted moments. "They're so young," she murmured, shaking her head. "I don't even want to think about them getting mated."

Ryan snorted. "No kidding. His reason was so that they could share each other's toys all the time."

A short laugh burst from her. Thank God that was the only reason Lucas had mentioned mating. They were still babies in her eyes.

"I kind of want to punch you right now," she blurted. Now that she understood the sexual frustration her sister had gone through with Ryan, she really wanted to punch him. And Aldric. Mainly Aldric, because her own sexual frustration was making her more than a little crazy. Frustrating alpha males.

He blinked. "Wait...what?"

"Never mind. Teresa here?"

He eyed her warily but shook his head. "No, she's at December's."

Which meant baby cuddle time. December and Liam's little girl was just five months old now. "See you later." She jumped off the front porch. Not only would she get to hold the new baby, she'd get baked goods because December was a baking machine.

"Tell Teresa to bring me back some cookies."

"Okay," she called over her shoulder.

She paused halfway across the expanse of land on her way to December and Liam's when she saw Gloria half-jogging toward her.

In jeans, knee-high black boots and a fitted black jacket, they were wearing pretty much the same thing. Except Natalia was wearing a pretty red and gold scarf Aldric had bought for her from QVC. She had a not-so-secret obsession with the shopping network and he'd surprised her last week.

"What's going on?" she asked.

"There's a vampire at the main house." Gloria slid her arm through Natalia's. "And I want to see him."

"A vampire... Oh, right, Niko. Why do you want to see him?"

It was pretty rare for a vampire to be at the ranch, but he'd needed to talk to Jayce about something. To do that, he'd had to ask Connor for permission to be on the ranch. Jayce could have met the male in town or somewhere else, but they'd been doing enough work together lately that Niko needed to speak with Connor and be accepted onto pack land. Because this was Connor's territory, period. While Jayce might technically not consider Connor his Alpha, anyone who came into this territory needed to clear it with the pack leader first.

"Not all of us get to go off on adventures." Gloria's voice was teasing. "I've never seen one up close and you know him, so you're taking me. I just want one peek, that's all."

Her sister was a beta and liked staying close to the ranch, to her pack. Natalia would have just gone to the main house if she'd wanted to see a vampire but she understood her sister was wired differently. It was part of her submissive nature.

"He's really nice. Not like other vampires I've met."

Gloria snorted. "Haven't most vampires you've met tried to kill you?"

"Good point. So...have you finished your Christmas shopping yet?"

Her sister shot her a sideways glance as they reached the front porch of Ana and Connor's home. "Christmas isn't until next month, you freak. And I swear to God if you tell me you're already done..."

"Then I won't tell you." Natalia did her shopping all year and was usually done by October. It made her sisters crazy.

"What did you get me?"

"I'm not telling," she said as the door opened and Leila, a seventeen-year-old shifter and enforcer-in-training, stepped out.

She grinned when she saw them. "Holy shit you guys, that vamp is hot!"

"He can hear you," Natalia murmured.

"I know." She was gone in a blur of motion, her long black hair flying behind her as she headed in the direction of her home.

"I don't remember being that insanely hormonal at her age."

Natalia snorted. "No kidding. I think she partially does it to mess with Jayce." The young shifter was having fun making him crazy.

Gloria blinked, took a step back to look at her.

Panic threaded through her veins. "What's wrong?"

"You said 'mess with' instead of 'fuck with.' What have you done with my sister? Have the pod people finally taken over?"

"Shut up. Vivian told me I had a potty mouth," she grumbled.

Gloria laughed as they stepped inside. "That sounds like her."

Natalia immediately scented Aldric, even before she heard that deep, sexy voice that made her completely crazy in the best way possible.

Seconds later they stepped into the entryway to find Connor leaning against the fireplace while Aldric and Niko sat on opposite couches. Natalia was about to introduce her sister to Niko when the male abruptly stood, staring at Gloria as if she was the best Christmas present he'd ever seen. His normally dark eyes started to glow a faint amber.

Okay, then. Natalia looked at her sister, surprised to find her staring at the male with blatant interest.

She cleared her throat at the sharp burst of lust that could have been emanating from either one of them. Or maybe both. "Gloria, this is Niko. Niko, Gloria."

Neither glanced at her but Niko strode forward and actually fucking bowed. Like some sort of old-school courtier, he took one of her hands, half-bowed and kissed it.

Natalia forced herself not to laugh as she went to sit in Aldric's lap. Seriously, what the hell was going on? She raised her eyebrows at Aldric who looked just as perplexed as her. Well that was good—at least that Niko didn't make a habit of doing... whatever it was he was doing.

Leaning close to Aldric's ear, she whispered low enough that only he could hear. "Is it just me, or is this a little weird that neither of them are talking?"

He let out a short laugh.

Connor cleared his throat, clearly ready to say something, when a little jaguar raced into the room, followed by a larger wolf.

Whatever was going on between Gloria and Niko, the spell seemed to be broken. Sort of. Her sister's cheeks were all flushed as she pulled her hand back.

Vivian meowed loudly, butting Niko's leg with her head.

Connor moved across the room lightning fast, picking the cub up in a protective gesture she understood. "She can smell that you're a vampire."

Whether Connor trusted the vamp or not wouldn't matter with a cub in the room. As Alpha, it was in his nature to protect the little ones. It was actually a shifter thing in general. And Niko was still fairly unknown to Connor, regardless of how much Jayce or she and Aldric trusted him.

Niko laughed. "Is she challenging me?"

"No, she wants you to pet her head." Connor's voice was wry. He held a wiggling Vivian in his arms. "This is Vivian, my daughter." There was a dark edge to his words, the indication clear. Make one wrong move and death would be swift and brutal.

Niko nodded, understanding. "I can leave now, if you'd prefer."

Connor looked at the male for a long moment, then set Vivian down, showing a huge amount of trust to this vampire. Though if the male even thought about making a wrong move, he'd be dead before he could act on it. She had that much faith in her Alpha's strength, knew how brutal he could be to his enemies.

Vivian started trying to climb Niko's leg, not using her claws as she batted at him. He bent down to pick her up but Lucas growled, watching Niko like a predator watched prey.

Natalia snorted. "Now *he* is actually challenging you." No doubt about that.

"Lucas, enough." Connor didn't raise his voice, didn't have to.

The pup stopped growling but stood close to Niko as he picked up Vivian and sat back on the couch. He looked out of place, the way he held her a bit awkward. To Natalia's surprise, Gloria scooped up Lucas and sat inches from Niko. She beamed at the male and started talking about the young. Her beta sister was acting out of character but it was clear to see why.

"It's like I've walked into the fucking Twilight Zone," she murmured to Aldric, who was also watching the show in fascination.

Vivian's head snapped toward Natalia and she let out a tiny roar.

Ah, hell. "Damn it, I'll put a dollar in the swear jar."

Vivian growled.

Crap, she'd said damn too. "Two dollars."

The little she-cat nodded then pounced from Niko's lap and sauntered out of the room as if she owned the place, her little tail swaying, Lucas not far behind her.

"She's a little extortionist," Natalia muttered.

Aldric snickered, his grip on her tightening. She loved the possessive way he held her. "Technically, she's not, since—"

"That's enough out of you." She nipped his jaw lightly, ready to get the heck out of there. She wanted alone time with Aldric in the worst way. Which gave her an idea... She turned to Niko, grinned. "Gloria's been telling me about this new restaurant in town she wants to try out."

Aaaaannnnd that was all the hint he needed.

The ancient vampire practically fell all over himself as he turned to her sister, asking if she'd like to go to dinner with him after he spoke to Jayce.

"Let's get out of here," she whispered to Aldric. She was done being patient and tonight was a full moon. They were bonding. Period.

"I'll catch up with you." His low voice wrapped around her, making her body flare to life. "Gotta talk to Connor about something."

Though disappointment slid through her, she nodded and headed out. Gloria and Niko stood too, leaving the house together as if no one else existed.

"What the fuck?" Connor stared after the two of them. "I've never seen anything like that."

"Swear jar, dude." Natalia gave Aldric one last kiss before following after the others. Instead of going in their direction, she headed back to her house.

She wasn't sure how long Aldric would be but by the time he got to their place she was going to make sure the waiting came to an end.

Chapter 33

Aldric stalked across the pack's property, energy pulsing through him in hard waves. He'd wanted nothing more than to toss Natalia over his shoulder like a fucking caveman and find the nearest quiet spot and fully claim her.

It was a full moon tonight and he was finally going to mark his mate, to bond with the female he loved more than anything. Life without her wasn't worth anything. The past month he'd finally courted her the way he should have all those months ago instead of acting like a fucking coward.

They were both ready now.

Still, he'd had to talk to Connor first, to let the male know that he had Aldric's full allegiance. That if he was called upon for anything, this was his pack now. His own brother didn't consider Connor his Alpha, but that was just the way the male was wired. Enforcers were a different breed. While it chafed Aldric a little to have an Alpha, the reward was worth it. A pack to call his own. And, more than that, it would make Natalia happy.

That was all he wanted. *She* was all he wanted. Now and forever. There was no doubt in his mind that she would leave her pack if he asked, but he could never do that. Her sisters and cousins lived here, she was happy here. And...he was happy too. A strange concept for someone who'd been a loner for so damn long. She made him want to put down roots.

He returned greetings to a few of the pack as he hurried to get to Natalia, but he didn't pause. When her house came into view he broke into a jog, instinct screaming at him to move faster, faster.

The moon urged him on, demanding he take his female. Nothing would get in their way or interrupt them. He'd called Gloria to let her know that he needed the house tonight and she'd been only too willing to stay out later with Niko.

It took all his restraint not to bust the door down like a maniac when he reached it. His skin felt too tight for his body, as if he could climb right out of it. The door was unlocked, no surprise. But once he was inside, he turned the deadbolt.

It snicked into place, the sound heavy in his ears. He was finally alone with his mate. He paused at a sound, realized water was running upstairs.

A deep-seated fear that he'd fuck this up simmered inside him, but he shoved it back down. He pushed aside all the voices that wanted to tell him he wasn't good enough for her, that he'd fail her. That once he admitted total and utter happiness, the universe would take her away from him.

She'd made him see differently. His female could take care of herself. And fuck it, a life without her simply wasn't worth living.

He followed that sweet, cherry blossom scent up the stairs. It called to him more than the sound of the shower.

All his muscles grew taut just thinking about her slick and naked, waiting in there for him. Over the last month he'd learned that she didn't care about a bed, she just wanted him.

Her desire for him humbled him. He needed her just as much but he loved knowing they were on the same wavelength, that their white-hot hunger mirrored each other's.

He stripped off his clothes as he took the stairs, not caring where he dropped them. As he reached her bedroom, he dropped his jeans, leaving them where they fell.

The door to the bathroom was open, steam billowing out. Beckoning to him along with her intensified scent.

His cock jutted in front of him, hard and eager as he silently stepped inside.

"Took you long enough." A hint of attitude punctuated her words.

God he loved her. "Impatient for me?" He stepped into the stone and glass enclosure, pulling the door shut behind him.

Natalia stood under the waterfall of jets, her espresso-colored hair seeming even darker when it was wet. Her deep brown eyes flared with heat as she drank him in from head to toe. "I'm very impatient... It's a full moon tonight." There was no trepidation in her words, just fire. As if she was daring him to say something.

"I know," he growled.

She reached for him, clutching onto his shoulders at the same time he reached for her hips. "You plan on telling me it's too soon or some other garbage, and I'll—"

"No." He bit the word out savagely. He wasn't waiting another day. Not even another fucking minute.

She blinked, as if she'd expected an argument. Then her mouth pulled into the sexiest, most satisfied grin. Without pause she grabbed onto his shoulder and hoisted herself up, wrapping her legs around his waist.

His thick cock was heavy between them. The feel of her slick body against his had all his senses going into overdrive. Simply looking at his female was enough to make him crazy, but feeling her like this and knowing she was about to be his for the rest of his life...

"I love you," she rasped out, raking her canines against his neck.

"Mine." It was all he could get out as he pinned her against the wall. He crushed his mouth over hers, taking, tasting.

He'd learned over the last month that his Natalia didn't need things sweet and soft. Sometimes she did, but she was a very sensual female.

Still...he pulled back a fraction. "Do you want our bed?"

In response she grabbed the back of his neck, pulled his mouth back to hers. *Thank fuck.* He didn't want to move from where they were.

She arched into him as their tongues tangled, her hard nipples brushing against his chest. Reaching between them, he palmed one, tweaked her nipple with his thumb and forefinger.

She moaned into his mouth, shuddering against him. Her fingers dug into his shoulders, her claws pricking at him.

He growled low in his throat, kissed a path from her mouth, along her jaw and down the column of her neck. His heart pounded out of control and his canines extended without thought, his wolf wanting to pierce her skin.

The need to mark her had all his primal instincts shoved to the surface, ready to take over.

"No going back." His voice was rough against her neck. He'd never thought he'd have a chance like this, a female like this.

"I don't want to." Her own voice was savage, laced with hunger. "Take me." A soft demand.

Though he hated to disentangle her from him, he moved them away from the wall. She dropped her legs and spun so that she was facing the wall. She placed her hands on it and looked over her shoulder at him, all fire and need as she pushed her ass back at him.

Water cascaded all around them, heat and steam billowing around them in a cocoon.

All the muscles in his body pulled tight as he drank in the sight of her.

He gently wrapped his hand around the front of her throat, turned her so that he could devour her mouth with his. She shoved her ass into him, arching and moaning as his tongue teased hers. It took willpower he didn't know he had not to just thrust into her.

This was her first time and it was their official bonding. That was the real reason he'd held off this past month—he'd wanted their first time together to be when they bonded forever. That final link where they committed to each other for always.

It should terrify him after failing his first mate, but the only thing that did scare him was the thought of a life without Natalia.

Sliding his other hand down her flat abdomen, he cupped her mound, slid his middle finger right over her pulsing clit.

"Aldric," she moaned.

"Say my name again." He sounded savage, even to himself. He kept his hand wrapped around her throat so she couldn't move as he oh so slowly began stroking her clit.

"Aldric." His name tore from Natalia's lips at his command. She jerked back against Aldric as he started teasing her. And he was definitely teasing. He had to scent how primed she was, had to know how ready she was for this. After a month of learning each other's bodies he knew her as well as she knew herself. And vice versa.

The only line they hadn't crossed was actual penetration. God, she was so ready for that. So ready her body was trembling out of control. Her inner walls clenched, empty, needy for him.

He growled softly against her neck, his canines grazing her pulse point as he worked his finger against her sensitive bundle of nerves. The way he held her, she could barely move.

The sensation of being immobile made this even more intense. She trusted him on every level, loved submitting to him like this. She was teetering right on the edge of pleasure, so close.

"In me," she rasped out, more plea than command.

He gave a low laugh, the sound dark and wicked against her neck. "Come first."

It was like his words set something off inside her. The orgasm that had been building rose higher and higher, crested as he increased his pressure against her clit. When she came she wanted him inside her.

That was what she desperately wanted, with a hunger she'd never imagined, barely understood. But her wolf knew that they needed to bond, connect on the most intimate level right freaking *now*.

She felt as if she'd die if he didn't push inside her.

As her climax surged through her, punching out to all her nerve endings, he dropped his hand from her neck, reached between her legs from behind. He delved two fingers into her slickness.

"So wet," he groaned.

She pushed back against him, not wanting fingers.

He withdrew and a second later she felt his cock nudge her entrance. She was still trembling from her orgasm, the pleasure too much and not enough.

Her inner walls tightened and she willed him to hurry up.

Slowly he pushed into her, inch by inch, filling her up. She reached back for him, grasping onto his hips as he stretched her. When he thrust fully inside her, she sucked in a breath. He cupped one of her hips and palmed a breast, teasing her nipple in slow, erotic strokes.

Breathing hard, she stilled, getting used to his size. The male was huge, perfect. Even so, she needed a second.

"Mine. Forever." He sounded savage, animal, even as he remained immobile inside her.

"Yours. Always," she whispered.

He jerked at her words, withdrawing just a fraction. She moaned at the friction. Oh yeah, that was what she wanted.

"Do something," she begged, drawing the word out.

He bit into her neck without actually piercing the skin, as if holding her in place. Then he began to move, thrusting his thick length into her at a steady pace.

At first.

The faster he slid in and out of her, the more erratic his thrusts became, mirroring the wild energy humming through her. She met him stroke for stroke.

A sharp flare of heat hit as his canines pierced her sensitive skin, right where her neck and shoulder met.

"Aldric," she screamed. Pleasure poured through her, overwhelming her, another orgasm wrenching her in its grip.

She slammed her palms against the tile wall as he continued thrusting. He pinned her up against it, taking more, possessing her completely.

There was no pain from the bite like she'd expected. Only pleasure.

He growled against her neck, his canines still in her skin, continued to thrust over and over until he growled hard and let go of her neck. He released himself inside her, a harsh groan tearing from him as he pulled her close, wrapping his arms tight around her.

As he buried his face against her neck, she leaned back into him, savoring his strength. She'd never felt more at home than with him, as if she belonged to him. And he to her.

Mine, mine, mine. She heard the words in her head.

Blinking, she jolted against him. A smile broke out over her face. Holy shit, they were truly bonded. Happiness exploded inside her, a kaleidoscope of colors in her mind. *Do you know another word besides mine?* she asked along their telepathic link.

He stilled. *I didn't realize I'd projected that to you... How do you feel?*

Perfect. It was true.

You're perfect.

Groaning, she arched against him. Though she was loath to move at all she wanted to see his face.

We're bonded. Awe tinged his voice. *I'll wear your mark.*

It took a moment to realize what he meant. She hadn't been thinking about that, hadn't been thinking about much after that orgasm. The gods or God or magic decided what mark the male wore. It was always a small tattoo-like symbol on their back or shoulder.

She twisted to face him and he pinned her flat against the tile wall. She wiggled against him. "I want to see it."

Looking down at her, his normally hard expression was soft, full of emotion. He gently let her go and turned.

Water continued to cascade around them, a steady stream of heat. She traced her finger over the small symbol on his upper shoulder, her heart swelling with love as she recognized what it was. "It's the Celtic symbol for everlasting love." Her voice cracked on the last word. Two triskeles were linked together, creating the everlasting circle of eternity.

He turned to face her again, pulled her into his arms in a tight, possessive grip. "I never imagined someone like you existed," he said softly. "You completely own me. Whatever you want is yours."

Her heart turned over. "I just want you. Forever."

"You've got me. All of me." He bent down slowly, brushed his lips over hers in a sensual kiss that made all her nerve endings sizzle.

Just like that, the familiar hunger he incited swept through her again and she knew they were in for a very, very long night.

This male was all hers. Hers to touch and kiss whenever she wanted. For always.

Epilogue

Holding a giant color wheel, a stack of design magazines and a basket of fresh-baked muffins, Natalia nudged the front door shut with her hip. She didn't bother locking it, not here on the ranch.

She followed the scent of her mate to the kitchen, where he was pouring a mug of coffee. Two of her favorite smells: coffee and Aldric.

Wearing low-slung jeans and no shirt, he took her breath away. Like usual.

The smile he gave her was slow, wicked. "Where'd you sneak off to?"

Natalia had gotten a call from December this morning that she'd baked, so while Aldric had been in the shower she'd hurried out to surprise him with breakfast. But then she'd been sidetracked by one of her brothers-in-law who needed help picking out a Christmas gift. "I'd hoped to be back before you got out."

Before she could set anything down, he took it from her and put it all on the center island. "December baked again?" he asked, pulling food from the basket.

"I promised her we'd watch Ellie tonight so they could get some grownup time." December and Liam had named their little girl Elspet after his long-deceased mother, but she was Ellie for short.

Watching the sweet baby wasn't an inconvenience, and she'd have done it without the baked goods anyway. Everyone in the pack looked out for each other and helped with the little ones when needed.

Aldric grinned at the news they'd be watching Ellie. At six months old, she was crawling everywhere. She hadn't had her first shift yet but she would soon enough. That was when the real fun would start. Pups were so mischievous and wanted to explore everywhere. "When do you want... pups?"

Hand halfway to the basket, she blinked. "I'm good waiting for a while." She stepped closer to him, wrapped her arms around his middle as he set his muffin down. "What about you?"

"Waiting is good for me too." He seemed almost relieved to admit it.

Over the last month they'd talked about everything under the sun—except kids. It had been intentional on her part, because after what he'd been through, Natalia hadn't wanted to rip open an old wound. Deep down she knew they should have discussed pups before bonding because it was a huge thing. But even if he hadn't wanted them, she'd have still mated him.

She cleared her throat. "You do want them though?"

His eyes widened slightly. "God, yes."

Relief slid through her veins at the vehemence in his voice. "Good. I'm selfish though. I want a few years of just us first." As shifters they had very long lifespans and she wanted some uninterrupted time with her bondmate.

"Me too." He brushed his lips over hers, then deepened the kiss.

She melted against him, her nipples beading tight against her bra cups as he lifted her up onto the island countertop. Forget breakfast, forget everything else. This male consumed her.

In a few weeks they'd have their own place. Just in time for Christmas. Since Aldric hadn't had a real Christmas in centuries she was going to make sure this one was special. That he knew just how loved he was and that the adventure for the two of them was just beginning.

Dear Readers

Thank you for reading the latest Moon Shifter book! If you'd like to stay in touch and be the first to learn about new releases you can:

Check out my website for book news:
   https://www.katiereus.com

Also, please consider leaving a review at one of your favorite online retailers. It's a great way to help other readers discover new books and I appreciate all reviews.

Happy reading,
Katie

Acknowledgments

As usual I owe a huge thanks to Kaylea Cross for helping me with the early version of this book. I'm also grateful to my editors, Deborah Nemeth and Julia Ganis for helping get this in shape. Thank you to Jaycee for creating such a wonderful cover. For my Moon Shifter readers who kept asking for Aldric and Natalia's story (and to see more of Jayce and Kat!) this one is for you. I'm also incredibly thankful to have such a wonderful assistant, Sarah, who takes on all the little (and big) things so I can get in more writing. For my family, thank you guys for putting up with my writing schedule. As always, thank you to God.

About the Author

Katie Reus is the *USA Today* bestselling author of the Red Stone Security series, the Ancients Rising series and the Redemption Harbor series. She fell in love with romance at a young age thanks to books she pilfered from her mom's stash. Years later she loves reading romance almost as much as she loves writing it.

However, she didn't always know she wanted to be a writer. After changing majors many times, she finally graduated summa cum laude with a degree in psychology. Not long after that she discovered a new love. Writing. She now spends her days writing paranormal romance and sexy romantic suspense.

Complete Booklist

Ancients Rising

Ancient Protector

Ancient Enemy

Ancient Enforcer

Ancient Vendetta

Ancient Retribution

Ancient Vengeance

Ancient Sentinel

Ancient Warrior

Ancient Guardian

Darkness Series

Darkness Awakened

Taste of Darkness

Beyond the Darkness

Hunted by Darkness

Into the Darkness

Saved by Darkness

Guardian of Darkness

Sentinel of Darkness

A Very Dragon Christmas

Darkness Rising

Deadly Ops Series

Targeted

Bound to Danger

Chasing Danger

Shattered Duty

Edge of Danger

A Covert Affair

Endgame Trilogy
Bishop's Knight

Bishop's Queen

Bishop's Endgame

Holiday With a Hitman Series
How the Hitman Stole Christmas

A Very Merry Hitman

MacArthur Family Series
Falling for Irish

Unintended Target

Saving Sienna

Moon Shifter Series
Alpha Instinct

Lover's Instinct

Primal Possession

Mating Instinct

His Untamed Desire

Avenger's Heat

Hunter Reborn

Protective Instinct

Dark Protector

A Mate for Christmas